Captain's Curvy Puck

C.H. James

Golden Storm Publishing

Captain's Curvy Puck – The Locker Room Series – Book Two

Paperback - First Edition

Cover designed by Golden Storm Publishing

Welcome to the Locker Room, where strong men & sports heroes find the curvy women of their dreams!

Miles Johnson

I lead the best hockey team in the country, and we're on track to re-write the record books. It's my final season; the body isn't what it used to be, but hockey means more to me than anything. Until she's around. I'm constantly distracted by the curvy beauty who's been put off-limits. She's Noah's little sister, and when he asks me to watch out for her, I can't help myself.
She's gorgeous. And that cute grin of hers has me coming back for more, even though I know I shouldn't.

Ellie Edwards

I'm the star player's little sister. I'm off-limits and it's always been that way.
Except for the captain. Miles Johnson. He pulls rank. His possessive alpha attitude has me breaking the ice to make him mine.

Our lust is hot and heavy. And then the unthinkable happens… Is he really going to want to settle down with a younger woman like me? Does he even want a family?

A steamy connection has these two opposites attracted instantly. But will the biggest surprise of all send him skating off into the distance?

Join the C.H. James Community!

STEAMY STORY. HAPPILY EVER AFTER. HOT HEROES.

GIVEAWAYS. FREE BOOKS.
WEEKLY NEW RELEASES.

Make sure you don't miss out on any of my new releases by signing up for my newsletter.
SIGN UP TO MY NEWSLETTER at https://bit.ly/chjamesnewsletter.

C.H. James
xoxo

CHAPTER ONE

Miles

I pull a deep gulp of my Budweiser, resting the cold bottle on my knee. The television blares loudly in front of me. The darkness of my dim living room makes the flashes of slow-motion replays even more eye-catching.

We fucking did it. Another win.

I take another sip as images of Parker Philips slapping home the fifth goal of the night plays out on the screen. The crowd roars on the TV and the camera pans to our leader, Coach Best. I chuckle, as the screen makes him look even more intense than in real life.

If Coach knew I had downed three beers already, he'd have me skating laps for hours.

I don't care.

I'm thirty-six years old, so I'm going to kick back on a Saturday night and drink a few fucking Buds if I want to.

Don't get me wrong, hockey is my number one priority. It always has been. Ever since I was twelve and I was drafted to the Edmonton Eagles. I made an instant impact, rising quickly through the team to make my senior debut at the prime young age of fourteen.

To this day, I'm still the youngest player to debut at the Eagles.

But when Canada's best team came in for me, there was no fucking way my dad, God bless his soul, would let me knock back the Vancouver Vikings. Not that I wanted to. They offered me big money straight off the stick. I don't care who you are - a few grand a week for a pimple-faced rookie is a lot of money.

And I haven't looked back since.

Four Stanley Cups. Five MVP awards. And my pride and joy, the Olympic Gold medal.

A smile creeps across my face as another goal flies in the back of the net. This time Noah Edwards slaps the puck home from a tight angle late in the third period. The camera zooms in on him, and then quickly pans to the crowd.

A sea of red and white rise from their seats, all clapping and cheering on the TV. I know it's only a replay, but still, a feeling of pride builds in my chest. Being the captain of Vancouver's favourite team is a privileged position. I can't walk anywhere in this city without being pulled aside for a selfie. Even on the rare occasions when I go to *The Bloody Viking,* the famous bar in the city centre, I'm mauled and harassed by drunk men and horny chicks all night.

Honestly, if it wasn't for the foul stench of the fans' breath, or the way the girls rubbed their plastic tits against me, I seriously wouldn't mind the attention.

Could I put up with it every minute of every day?

Hell no!

Why the fuck do you think I'm sitting in my living room on a Saturday night all alone?

But I understand. I'm a hockey fan, too. Even I get all fan-girl crazy when I see Wayne Gretsky and Mario Lemieux at the end-of-season award functions. The first time I met *The Great One,* I was in the bathroom of the Ritz Palace in London. I was so excited that I forgot I was pissing at the urinal and let go of my cock. I peed all over his shoes and ruined a very expensive pair of leather Oxfords.

We joke about it now, but believe me, it was awkward between us for a while.

The last dregs of my beer slide down my throat. The final buzzer blasts, and I watch Noah Edwards pick up yet another man of the match award. That's eleven this season – he's favourite to defend his MVP title, and deservedly so.

I scooch forward in my armchair, pressing my knees to head into the kitchen to fetch a fourth beer. As I feel my knees creak beneath my hands, I'm stopped mid-way by the image of a gorgeous, curvaceous woman on the television screen.

"Ellie…"

The name leaves my lips like a breath of fresh air.

A twist in my stomach forces me to stand tall, my eyes fixed on the screen. Noah's twin sister, Ellie Edwards, is cheering from the stands. Her lips are red and glossy – they look as plump, chapped and kissable as ever. Her dark, chocolate brown hair is as smooth as it always is, shining in the flashing lights of the Viking Arena. I love her hair… The way it flows down her body, long and elegant towards her busting cleavage.

I feel my cock twitch, but before I can reach down, she's gone. Ellie's perfect face is replaced by two men in suits. They're not even close to being as good looking as Ellie. They're holding microphones and talking passionately about yet another impressive win for the Vikings and it's enough to force me to spin around.

I grunt and turn to retreat to the fridge, the image of Ellie's tits stirring inside my head. I reach for the final beer in the coldness of my bare fridge and when I pop the cap, I hear my phone buzzing in on the table.

I run back, sucking a deep gulp of the fresh fizz of the lager.

"Hello?" I grab my phone and swipe without looking.

"Miles, bro!" A deep voice shouts, though a mix of background noise is making it hard to hear. "Are you there? Hello?"

"Yeah, I'm here," I say, pulling my phone to look at the screen. I see 'Noah' as the caller and when I push the phone back to my ear, a loud smash clatters. "Noah? Is that you? Is everything ok?"

"Bro! I can't really hear you," Noah's voice yells, another smash of glass rattling my eardrum. "I need you to come down to the bar. It's fucking crazy here tonight and I might need some help keeping things under control."

I slurp my drink and look down at my comfy black trousers with a deep sigh. I'm also wearing my favourite Beatles shirt. It's the shirt I wear when I want to be comfy. It's my go-to top when I'm sure I'll be laid back on the sofa all night. It's so fucking old the cotton is soft and worn down. It's the softest fucking thing I've ever felt. I don't care if it's faded and got holes in it… It's. Fucking. Comfy.

"Oh, man…" I drag out. "Are you sure you can't handle it? I'm settled in for the night, man."

The phone fumbles and I hear girly screams and deep roars of wild hockey fans. There's chanting and by the sounds of it, someone has one of those Vikings horns and is using it in a sculling contest. Without him even saying, I know where Noah is. There's no other place in the city that has people who makes noises like that.

The Bloody Viking.

It's the place to be for hockey fans.

"Miles! Are you there?" Noah's voice comes back to the phone. "Seriously, I need to go. Some weird chick has straddled Jamie Fisher. Bro, when you get here… Find Ellie."

My stomach drops at the mention of his twin sister's name.

Ellie's there…

"…she's disappeared and I can't look for her." Another fumble echoes in my ear, but I'm already racing up the hallway to change my pants when I hear Noah's final words, "I'll see you when you get here."

I grab the first pair of jeans on the floor of my bedroom. Stepping across to my wardrobe, I pluck a white hoodie and race out of the front door of my apartment, only stopping to slide on the closest pair of shoes to the door.

One of the benefits of being a pro-hockey player is I get paid handsomely. I can afford a downtown apartment, and as I sprint up the dark streets of late-night Vancouver, I've never been more grateful for that.

I turn the final corner and my chest heaves at the sight of at least thirty bodies loitering outside of *The Bloody Viking*. You know it's a busy night when there's a line-up to get inside. And that normally spells trouble.

I'm coming, Ellie. I'm coming.

My untied laces act as a hazard as I sprint harder and faster at the sight of the busy bar, but I don't bother to tie them. Even if I fell face first in a pile of snow, I'd have the possibility of Ellie's safety being at risk to pick me straight back up again. I can't afford to have her alone. Not for one second. Not tonight. Not any night.

I reach the front door of the bar. Two bouncers are holding the line of impatient drunks waiting to get inside. A group of guys at the front recognize me and start shouting out for an autograph.

I'm too focused on the bouncers. I work my way around the line of people, finally reaching the front of the line.

"You've got to let me in," I breathe, gripping the biggest bouncer by the jacket. It's a weird feeling being bigger and bulkier than a nightclub bouncer, and I'm sure if it came down to it, I could take both of these fuckers at the same time.

"Miles Johnson?" The bouncer smiles, his eyes bright. A hot breath of steam leaves his smiling mouth as he turns to his buddy and then back to me. "You don't need to wait in line, big guy. Come in!"

He grips the red rope that's blocking the door, unhooks it, and pushes the door of *The Bloody Viking* open. I offer a quick smile as thank you, but there's only one thing I want right now, and that's to find…

"Ellie?"

CHAPTER TWO

Ellie

"Baby!" I squeal, skipping across to Miles. "I knew you would come!"

Miles' face is stern. He steams across to me and instantly wraps his arms around my body, glaring around the packed bar with narrowed brows. Warmth fills my insides, and I fall into his firm grasp as if I'm weightless.

Miles. My safe place.

"Where's Noah?" Miles says, releasing his hold enough so I can look up at him.

My mind goes blank as I stare up into those intoxicating golden eyes. Miles' face remains hard, but his eyes are soft on me. They always are. I allow myself to sink into his chest once more, drawing in his masculine scent. I feel his firm chest against my cheek, his heart racing inside his body. He's panting, out of breath, like he's been rushed inside.

The way he's gripping me so tightly is making his ripped arms tense against me. He's owning me, just like he always did. Without even seeing it, I know he's eyeballing every guy in this place, warning them off me.

Miles Johnson. Captain of the Vancouver Vikings. And my brother's teammate.

"Ellie?" Miles' deep voice rumbles inside his chest. "Where's Noah and the guys?"

The guys.

I've been around hockey players my entire life. My older brother, Noah Edwards, is the National Hockey League's hottest player. It's been that way for years now, and I'm used to living in his shadow.

I don't mind, though.

I don't want fame or stardom.

I'm happy working as a waitress in a coffee shop. I'm okay with my role as the 'other twin'. I'm the fat sister, and after years and years of playing that role, I've accepted it with opens arms.

What I don't like, though, is when the guy I've crushed on for years, Miles, finally has me in his arms and his first question is *'where are the guys'.*

"Do you want to get a drink?" I say, ignoring the question of the whereabouts of the guys.

A pair of panties flies across the room and lands on Miles' shoulder. Shrieks of laughter from a group of girls across the room makes my hands curl, and when Miles sees, he simply pulls me in closer.

Shaking his head, Miles swipes away the red lace from his shoulder and we move towards the bar. We dodge bodies and wet splashes of spilling beer as Miles parts the crowd. He's a foot taller than most of the other patrons and I glide through the crowd under Miles' arm.

We find a space at the front of the bar and I rest my head on Miles' shoulder.

My legs are trying to skip. My face won't stop beaming. I'm so fucking happy that Miles is here. His heavy arm is pulling me into him in a way that has me under his control.

And I like it.

I've had a huge crush on Miles ever since I saw him. I was fourteen, and Noah had just made the team and our entire family was welcomed into the Vikings crew.

Being one of the oldest guys on the team, Miles didn't notice me until my twenty-first birthday.

Noah had buddied up with Miles by then and he dragged him along to my birthday dinner. The attraction across the table was instant. I fooled myself for years after that night. I was convinced there was no way that a huge, handsome, bulky hockey player like Miles Johnson would want a curvy, lumpy-in-all-the-wrong-places girl like me.

He could have any girl he wanted, right? Why the hell would he want a plus-size chick like me?

Now, don't get me wrong… I'm not ashamed of my body. Heck, I *own* these tits. And my ass? I'm sorry skinny chicks, but you've got nothing to back up onto a healthy, long, hard dick like I do. The feeling of my ass cheeks bouncing on a guy while he's fucking me from behind… I've had guys coming within seconds while they gawk at my body, astonished at the way my ass moves.

But with Miles? Nothing happened for a few years between us. From a distance, we would smile, wink and flirt from opposite sides of the room.

Until one summer night at a hockey function in Toronto.

Miles had lost out to a rookie player from New York in the All-Star line-up of the year. For the first time in seven years,

Miles wasn't an All-Star player. They say it was the moment his career started to decline; age was finally catching up with him. It's bullshit of course, Miles is still a top athlete.

But that night… That night he was so fucking pissed that he stormed outside and started ripping out the small trees that lined the pathway.

I went after him. Unlike anything I'd ever done before that moment of my life, I took a shot. In the privacy of the dark night sky of Toronto, I leaned up and kissed him, hoping to hell it might calm him down. It did. And the sparks were instant.

I've been determined to make him mine ever since.

"Just a beer, thanks, Greg," Miles says, leaning his forearms against the edge of the bar. He turns to face me, and for the first time, he smiles.

"Oh, there it is…" I tease, tracing a finger along his lips.

"Shut up. I was worried about you," Miles concedes, his brows finally relaxing.

I step in closer, feeling the warmth radiating off Miles' body. Two beers slide across in front of us and Miles picks his up and downs half of it in a single gulp.

"Aren't you a sweetie?" I walk a finger up his chest, and when Miles twists his neck around towards the packed bar room, I recognise the searching look. He's looking to see where my brother is. "Don't worry. He's in the back room playing eight ball."

"We should go back there then… He called me." Miles says, his topaz-coloured iris splitting my insides with a handsome stare.

"He called you?"

"Yeah," Miles shrugs, sipping his beer. "Said it was fucking crazy down here tonight." A loud roar is timely, and when a guy props up on another man's shoulders and starts chugging a beer, I can't help but smile. "And he wasn't wrong."

"They're celebrating! Everyone in town is talking about the game." The entire bar erupts with a loud chant. The guy floating on someone's shoulders finishes the beer-filled Viking horn to a rapturous applause and there's beer flying everywhere. "You realise you just beat the second-placed team in the conference *seven-zero.*"

Miles sneaks a cocky smile, before the captain inside of him takes hold and pulls his features down. "It's just one game. We're only one step closer to the goal we set ourselves. We haven't won anything yet. It's gonna take a hell of a lot more than that to win this championship, so we can't afford to get ahead of ourselves."

Oh fuck, my ovaries.

There's something special about a rough, tall, Canadian talking hockey. It's passion, strength and pure masculinity all rolled into one pussy-drenching conversation. And when the guy who's speaking looks the way Miles does, fuck... My panties soak through in an instant.

"Oh, Miles..." I sneak in closer, so my hip pops into him with a cheeky poke. "You know how much I love it when you talk hockey to me..."

I see the flash across Miles' eyes. He fades into a far, far away land... I know he can see my naked body in his trance. It's right there in front of him. Standing and waiting for him to take me as his own. My body is his. He knows it. I've let him fuck me like a wild, ravaged animal before. He's let me explore every ripple of his toned stomach. I've licked fudge from his body and eaten strawberries from his mouth while he smashes two fingers deep inside me.

Our sex is hot, steamy, and passionate.

Is it because it's forbidden? Is it because Noah doesn't know?

Not for me. I don't care if my brother finds out. It's Miles who cares about that.

No. For me, it's our connection. My body *craves* Miles. It's made for him. And he's made for me.

"Well, you know, baby…"

Miles leans in close, his teasing, lustful voice tickling my ear-lobe. A shiver of excitement rolls down my arm, allowing me to loop a finger into the hook of his jeans. Just as Miles dips his head towards my neck, giving in to every temptation he's been fighting, a hand grips his shoulder and pulls him back with a forceful yank.

"There you two are!" My brother's voice bellows.

Miles' eyes shoot open, and my finger unhooks from the belt loop of his jeans. I take a subtle step back and sip my beer, eyeing Noah's smoky grey eyes over the top of my glass with a scowl only a sibling could get away with.

"Hey, Bud," Miles says, his voice so fake and un-casual I'm sure Noah will think something's up. Not that I care, I've been telling Miles we should just tell my brother we're screwing for months. "It's fucking noisy in here, right? Your sister was having trouble hearing me."

Your sister? Your sister???!!!

Noah nods and they chat casually for a moment, but I'm not listening. A ball of fire is building in my belly, and it's not the usual one that Miles ignites inside of me.

Did Miles really just refer to me as 'your sister'?

I know he's nervous about revealing whatever the hell this is that's going on between us… But surely I'm worthy of more than that?

"Come on, Ellie," Noah says, waving his arm so I follow behind them. "The rest of the team are back here. Security keeps a better eye on the crowd up this end, so if anything starts up-"

"I think I'm just going to go home," I shrug. Miles' face drops and he stops still. "I'm a bit tired and I-"

"You're tired?" Noah says, his eyes darting between Miles and I, surprise in his expression. "I never thought I'd hear those words come out of your mouth. My sister… The party girl… Tired?"

I shrug, my arms folded over my chest. Miles is trying to catch my eyes, but his newest pet name for me is still rattling around in my head.

Your sister. Seriously?

"Yeah. Well. There you go."

"Oh, well…" Noah breathes heavily and presses his hands to his hips. A smash of several glasses from behind the bar cause the entire bar to erupt in a wicked cheer that lasts several seconds, and when they die down, Noah moves towards the front door of the bar. "Come on, I'll wait with you until a taxi picks you up."

Noah moves ahead, and as he does, I see the panic in Miles' eyes.

"I can wait with her," Miles says, his voice desperate as he side-eyes me. Noah spins on the spot and looks at his teammate. "Yeah, I mean, I didn't really want to be here anyway… I only came because you called…"

There's a silence. Normally, I don't mind waiting by myself, but as annoying and demoralising as it is, I don't really feel like waiting in the freezing cold snow for a taxi all alone. Vancouver is safe, of course, but you just never know which creep might be lurking around the corner.

Noah looks at me and then at Miles. He does it another two times and I swear there's a twin moment going on right here. I *feel* it. It's like my brother is speaking to me through our minds.

Noah suspects something is going on between Miles and I. And whether it's that he doesn't want to believe it, or whether he *can't* believe it, I'm not sure. All I do know is that he doesn't give a shit. So if he doesn't care, then why the hell does Miles?

"Are you ok to go with Miles?" Noah asks, his large hand clutching my shoulder in a big-brotherly way.

"It wouldn't be the first time," I say, my face bright.

Noah hums and then flashes a hardened look to his captain. "Look after my sister, ok?"

"I always do," Miles says, as if he's trying to convince Noah.

With a nod, Noah leaves and I'm being led through the crowd and out of *The Bloody Viking.*

CHAPTER THREE

Miles

"Ellie! Ellie!" I pace through the crowded streets directly outside of the bar, trying to keep up. "Wait, please!"

Fuck.

I know I've said the wrong thing. The second the words left my lips, I felt it. My heart sank, and panic ripped through my body. I knew I just had to get her alone. If I could just explain myself, maybe the scowl might fade and everything would be ok again.

I *need* everything to be ok again.

I don't know what my fucking problem is. Despite how I feel about Ellie, the thought of telling one of my best friend's that I'm banging his sister scares the shit out of me.

I'd rather fight a seven-foot, toothless goaltender any day rather than have that conversation.

I catch up to Ellie, and she turns to face me. Her usually bright and bubbly eyes are blank. Her gorgeous hair flows in the gentle breeze that's making my cheeks prickle in the cold night air. She's not smiling, and that alone kills a part of me.

"Sweetie," I pant, gripping her by the wrists. "Listen…"

"What is it?" Ellie barks, cutting me off with her snappy tone. "Why do we have to keep hiding? I'm tired of it, Miles."

"I know you are…" I gulp down, my hands sweating like never before.

"What is it? You tell me you're not embarrassed…"

"And I'm not! That's not it at all." My voice is rising, a barrel of hot steam coming from my mouth with every word. "I swear on my father's grave, I'm not ashamed to be with you, Ellie Edwards."

Why anyone would ever be embarrassed to be with a goddess like Ellie, I don't know.

She's been hurt before. I know that. Maybe that's why she's so sensitive about me not wanting to tell Noah? Maybe that's why this means so much to her?

She's told me all about *Kelvin* and his stupid excuses about why he never took her anywhere. Even when they did go out, he didn't hold her hand or display any form of affection around other people. It's not just that… There's more to *Kelvin,* and I swear to God, if I ever see that piece of shit, I'ma smack him like the tiny little black puck he is.

Ellie folds her arms across her chest and sighs. A gut-wrenching feeling pulls at me, and I force myself to take a timid step forward and pull her into my arms.

This woman is gorgeous. She's everything a woman should be. Her body is a wonderland. A curvy ride that I've had the pleasure of seeing every inch of. But she's so much more than a sexy stunner that gets my balls bursting with the slightest touch.

It's her laugh, that infectious giggle that tickles my ears so often. She's so easy going and relaxed. She's happy. Like, way over-the-top happy, and that's an amazing trait to have in this horrible dark world.

That why I know for her to react the way she has, I've fucked up big time.

Ellie sinks into me and I feel her breathe me in. Her body rises and falls in my arms, and for a moment, it's like nothing has happened. I haven't put my large hoof in my mouth.

I draw in a breath of her peach-scented hair and it's the connection that's between us that calms the situation.

It's the heat. The passion. *The love.*

It's tugging and rippling through our bodies, prying at our emotions to forgive and move on. I've never felt this way about anyone. Heck, I'm not sure I've felt like this about anything in my life, and that includes hockey.

But to move on, I need to do the right thing for this girl, and fucking man up.

I pull Ellie by the chin so her deep, leafy green eyes latch on. A brisk breeze is growing restless around us, and flakes of snow begin to dot the dark night sky with tiny flecks of white. I feel her body against mine, and my twitching dick reminds me that it's been five long weeks since I've had her all to myself.

Five weeks too long.

"Babe…" I feel Ellie breathe deeply under my touch. "I'll tell him. If that's what you want… If you're ready for that, I'll tell him."

Ellie's glossy lips curl upward, only, I was expecting more of a smile than she's giving me. I wanted a leap in the arms, smack-a-kiss on the mouth reaction… Instead, Ellie is barely smiling, and when she looks up again, a frown forms across her brow.

"So…" Her voice is soft, hauntingly beautiful as always, but I can tell there's more to this conversation that I didn't anticipate. "What exactly are you telling him? Because… Knowing my brother as I do, I don't think '*hey buddie, I'm banging your sister three ways til Sunday…*' will go down so well…"

I shuffle on the spot, looking at my untied laces and then up again. "Well, I guess I'll just ease him into it."

Ellie links her arms around my neck and pulls herself up, her breasts rubbing against my chest. Her body feels perfect against mine, but it's just making me want her even more. Ellie's mouth moves close to mine, and the heat of her breath sends shivers down my spine.

"Spunky-monkey…" Ellie says, her favourite nickname sounding weirdly odd outside of the bedroom. "Would you like me to tell him?"

I shake my head firmly. "No. No way. I'm the man and I'll be the one to take the hit."

"This isn't hockey…"

"It doesn't matter. Leave it to me. I'll deal with it."

The moment the words leave my mouth, a bright flash stings my eyes and lights up the darkness around us. It's bright and blinding, only, before I can react, the light is gone.

Ellie gasps beside me, and she's crouched down with her arm over her face. Instinctively, I jump across shield her behind my body. I cover her, protecting her from the danger of the unknown. *No one hurts my girl.*

My eyes squint, seeking the source of the flash. It's my ears that come to life first, though. A cackling laugh echoes off the buildings of the dark streets, and surrounds us on the sidewalk with a disgusting merriment.

"Who the fuck is there?" I call out, my voice dense.

A bright red blur is slowly fading in my eyes, and the intensity of the flash that's temporarily blinded me in the pitch-black darkness is disappearing. Ellie pokes her head around, but I ensure she's protected with my arm holding her back.

"Stay back, baby," I say.

As Ellie's fingers grips into my back, I see a tiny man with wiry hair and glasses. He's smiling brightly a few feet away from us, staring down at a camera that's looped around his neck. His laugh is high-pitched. No shit, I've heard catfights that sound nicer than this horrid, wickedly painful snigger.

"Hey! What the fuck do you think you're doing?" I growl, my hands curling into fists.

My heart races inside my chest, and I stand tall to protect Ellie. This man looks harmless, not to mention he's about three feet shorter than I am, but you can never be too careful. He might be carrying a knife or a gun, or worse, he might be a Toronto fan.

"Oh! I'm going to make a fortune!" The man cries, his tiny voice echoing in the darkness. "Miles Johnson has a lady friend! And I've got the first picture!"

I march across and slap the camera from the man's hand. It crashes to the sidewalk and shatters. I grab a fistful of his coat and twist, lifting his shaking body from the ground. I pull him to eye level, leaving his legs dangling like a frog in a net.

"You pricks think you can just go around taking pictures of whoever you want," I growl, my nostrils snorting.

"Babe! Stop!" Ellie steams up beside me, her voice desperate. "You can't hurt him. You've got more to lose than he does."

The stupid man's brows waggle in front of my nose. He's sneering and the pathetic look on his face is making my blood boil. I grip tighter and give him a hard shake that makes his keys fall out of his pocket. I'm fuming. I make damn sure my knuckles dig into his chest with every thrust I shake his body with.

"Miles! Come on!"

Ellie tugs at my arm and fuck me if she isn't stronger than she looks. I release my fist and let the asshole fall in a heap on the cold, hard concrete. The adrenaline racing through my veins makes me kick out at him as he reaches for his keys. Luckily for me, I don't connect because Ellie's pulling me away.

"Get in," Ellie says, pushing me backwards and into a taxi.

"What about the picture?" I say, my voice hard and raised. I wince at myself and make a mental note to never use that tone towards Ellie again. When she raises her brows at me, I take a deep breath and force myself to calm down. "The picture, babe. He'll sell it. It'll be worth a fucking fortune."

"So?" Ellie shrugs, her hands gripping mine across the back seat of the taxi. "Let him. It doesn't matter."

"But it'll be all over tomorrow's papers. Every website in the fucking world will have us locked arm in arm on the sidewalk on their front page…" I say, my eyes feeling as if they're going to pop out at any second. "Doesn't that bother you?"

Ellie looks up to the roof of the taxi as if the answer is written in chewing gum up there.

"Hmmm… Let me think about that for a second…" Ellie chimes, her face so bright I'm sure a magic spell was waved over her at birth, making her the most beautiful woman ever. "Nope. I don't care. The people who read those gossip magazines are low-life idiots anyway."

"Like the wanks who get the content for them then?" I growl, picturing that smug prick with stupid glasses.

"Exactly." Ellie nods, leaning across to peck my cheek with a kiss that sends a prickling heat to my heart. "But… We do have one problem."

I frown. "Oh yeah? What's that?"

"Noah reads the paper every day."

CHAPTER FOUR

Ellie

M iles pays the taxi driver and we're racing up the dark stairwell of his downtown apartment. Miles hustles ahead of me, taking the stairs two at a time. I sneak a quick look at his cute butt as he lunges, and when I try to reach out for a cheeky backhanded slap, I miss and stumble forward.

"Oh, shit!" I laugh, catching my fall with my palms.

"What are you doing? Are you ok?" Miles turns around, eyes wide. He retreats down and helps me up, guiding me back to my feet with two strong hands.

I look up, giggling. "Yes, I'm fine. I was trying to do this." I reach around and give his tight backside a squeeze and wiggle my brows. "It's too sweet to resist. But the stairs kind of got in the way."

"Come on," Miles chuckles and rolls his eyes. He grips my hand and leads the way forward, a skip in his step.

"Remind me again why we're hurrying?"

We reach the top of the stairs of the third level. The corridor is dark, the only light guiding us is tiny orange wall-lamps spaced out every few feet. I've been here a few times, but usually Miles would be attached to my mouth as we stumbled up the corridor.

"I don't want Noah to find out about us from anyone else…"

Miles plucks his keys from his pocket and unlocks the door to apartment fourteen. The familiar smell of apple and cinnamon floats through the doorway and meets my smiling lips. Miles might be tough and burly on the outside… After all, his reputation on the ice is one of physical brutality and unforgiving strength… But once you see how he lives; candles, potpourri and soft throws over his sofa, you get a personal insight into the heart of this gorgeous man.

I smile, looking around his living space. A new turquoise coloured blanket draped over the arm of the grey sofa is a new touch. Smiling, I can't help but notice the collection of travel magazines scattered on the glass coffee table and wonder over to check them out.

"Planning a trip?" I grab the top brochure and flick through the pages. "Luxury in New York, hey? Damn, these are some nice places."

"Huh? Wha-" Miles is busy fumbling around in the pocket of his coat, and when he looks up to see me with the brochure, a look of surprise makes his eyes pop. "Oh, that… Yeah…" I sense a hint of hesitation in his voice and his eyes keep flicking from me to the floor. "End of season holiday or something… Perhaps."

"I hope you were planning on inviting me! I've never been to New York before… I could visit Hazel!" I bounce on my heels, clapping the brochure between my hands. "She's always going on about this little bakery she loves… We could save money and stay with her, do you-"

"Ah… Ellie?" Miles strides across the room, his coat now on the hook, revealing a cute Beatles shirt that looks as old as me.

"I'm going to call Noah. I need to get it off my chest. I won't be able to sleep if I don't."

Miles' cheeks are flushed red and as he moves in closer, I notice tiny beads of sweat forming across his brow. *This really means something to him.* I take a second to draw a long breath, smiling softly to Miles who is shaking. I take his hands in mine, lean up and peck a soft kiss to his lips.

My heart leaps. It's screaming out for me to latch on and taste him right here, right now. I want to tackle him to the sofa and pull his cock out, slap it against my tongue and taste it all for my own.

Miles' hand curls around my back, and I allow my head to fall on his chest, releasing the naughty dream floating through my mind. He pulls tight, holding me like he's never going to let me go. Or maybe he's holding me like it might be the last time he gets to? Maybe he thinks Noah will forbid our love.

Miles is such a decent, loyal guy, that if Noah said he didn't like it, he would give him the respect of distancing himself from me. Despite our connection.

Fuck.

A pull grabs my stomach and yanks down.

That can't happen. I won't let it happen.

"Just send him a message…" I shrug lazily. "It'll be quicker."

"I can't do something this huge over text message…"

"Of course you can! And it's not fucking huge!" I say, my voice begging to be listened to. I push back against Miles' chest, grab his phone from his hand and tap out a message. My tongue slides between my teeth as I type quickly, passing the phone back to Miles before I hit send. "Read it. Then press send if you're happy. I'm tired and I want this to be over already."

I study Miles' eyes as they move across the screen. After a few seconds, he closes his eyes and I see his finger tap on the screen. A 'woosh' blasts from his phone, confirming he's hit send.

A bright smile lights up my face and I pull Miles into my gaze with a dip of my head.

"It's done now…" I say.

Before I can say another word, a bing makes us both jump. I'm shaking, and when Miles looks up, he's as white as a ghost.

"Want me to read it?" I hold my hand out, my expression soft.

Miles nods and passes me his phone. He steps back and spins on the spot, his hands running through his sandy blonde hair as he draws in deep, long breaths.

I look down, and read Noah's reply out aloud:

No shit, mate. You guys haven't exactly been hiding it well. Just treat her right. I'd hate to have to kick my captain's ass.

Miles spins on the spot. His smile lifts his cheeks and the way he's holding me is like a giant Noah-shaped weight has been lifted off his shoulders. With his eyes trailing down my body, Miles takes one giant step and lifts me up.

"Argh! Miles!" I squeal, giggling. Miles spins on the spot, twirling me like I'm a little fucking girl again. "See! I fucking told you."

Miles drops me to the floor and presses a quick kiss to my forehead. "I should never have doubted you, sweetie."

I smile in agreement. "Nevermind. You will learn. Now…" I trail a teasing finger along Miles' chest and drop it to the button of his jeans. His eyes pop and I swipe a teasing tongue across my lips. "Can we go to bed already?"

Miles growls and sweeps down to bite down on my lip. "Why go to bed when we can just do it here?"

"Very true… I've been patient, ever since you walked into the bar looking all serious and sexy…" His lips suck mine, pulling me closer. His mouth locks, pressing hard against my mouth and I can feel the relief as his tongue glides inside my mouth.

"You like me coming to save you?" Miles pulls away, his eyes heavy and deeply fucking sexy.

"Mmmmhmmm…"

I moan softly. My hands fall down to unbutton his pants and they drop to the floor. The warmth of the living room rises as our movements increase with rapid speed. My cheeks flush hot and they're burning as hot as my pussy. Miles dips to my neck and sucks hard against my sensitive skin. His hands roam my body, grabbing every bump and curve that I know drives him wild while he bites down on my neck.

"Oh, shit…" Miles breathes. "I've missed this body."

I dip inside the waistband of his underpants and grip his hard length. *Holy Moly. I forgot how fucking big it is.* Miles moans loudly, grabbing my tits beneath my thick jumper, searching for my stiffened peaks. His mouth pulls back as he rests his forehead on mine and swipes a soft finger over my nipple.

I stroke, long and hard along his pulsing cock, sneaking a look down at his perfect looking dick. I've seen dicks of all shapes and sizes… But this behemoth is the best I've ever had.

It's pointing up at me. The single eye is staring at me, begging to be tasted. Wet precum is glistening on the tip, teasing my mouth as Miles groans in my ear.

"You like that, don't you, Big Boy?" I whisper seductively, stroking long and slow.

My heart races inside my chest. Blood heats every nerve, sending tingling sensations down to my soaked pussy. My palm grips Miles harder and I reach with a second hand to glide up and down his long length.

My full strokes have him gasping with his head rolled back. I'm using both arms, like I'm pumping a fucking water tank or something. Two hands is what it takes to wrap this cock, and my body is aching to have him inside of me.

I watch with hooded eyes, his sandy hair shagging in his eyes as his breathing deepens. I feel my panties soaking through and my body is aching for him to touch me. But I can wait. The way his body is twisting and jerking with every movement my hands wrap around his girth, circling and stroking simultaneously is enough pleasure for me right now.

"Fuck… Baby…" Miles groans.

"Yeah, you like that? You like me stroking your big cock, baby?"

Miles pops one eye open and looks down at me. He struggles to allow properly formed words to leave his lips, "Fuck yes, baby."

I drop to my knees and Miles grips my hair, looking down with his cheeks flaming.

Excitement floods my core as I stare at his long shaft, my fingers gripping every inch of his engorged flesh. My mouth is wet and when I kneel up and lather a pool of saliva along his shaft, making my hand glide faster up and down, I feel his bulge swell.

I want to suck his perfect length, but he's right on the edge and if I keep doing what I'm doing, his orgasm will be satisfying enough to see.

"Come for me, baby…"

"What…" Miles tries to speak, but with every stroke I slide he's gripping my hair harder and harder. "You… What… About… You…."

I feel his cock throb and I know he's close. My tongue is begging to taste him, but it will have to wait.

"There's time, baby. Just let go…"

As the words leave my lips, Miles moves his hands around the back of my head and he's hunched over, his mouth gasping for breath. His hips jerk and I stroke harder, the feeling of his cock growing firmer before a final release has white ropey shoots of pleasure hot on my lips.

"OHHHH!!"

Miles' cock releases hot pleasure and tickles my tastebuds as I swipe my tongue across my lips, opening my mouth and looking up at Miles with lust hooding my eyes. He looks down at me, and a grunting chuckle makes me laugh.

I see the relief in his golden gaze. The weight of guilt that fucking his teammates sister brings is gone.

Finally.

CHAPTER FIVE

Miles

Bacon splatters in the pan. A splash of oil flies onto my stomach, burning my belly with a hot singe.

"Fuck!" I pat at my stomach, quickly grabbing the tea towel and dabbing at the spot.

"Is everything ok in here?" Ellie says through a yawn.

My jaw drops, and suddenly the pain has died away.

"Holy shit…" I say, my voice crawling across to Ellie who's dressed in nothing but skimpy panties and my old hockey jersey. "Baby, you look so fucking sexy."

I glide across and sweep Ellie into my arms. She falls into me, and I allow her body to dip and drop close to the floor. She's supported only by my arm and I smother a deep kiss to her soft, plump lips.

"Well, good morning to you, too," Ellie says, her eyes tired.

Another loud crackle and splatter has me retreating to the frying pan and Ellie follows, wrapping her arms around my stomach from behind. After tending to the vicious bacon, I turn to face her.

Her cheeks are flushed with a hint of pink. Her eyes definitely look tired, but we were up all night… It's as if she's flushed or unwell.

"Watch it," I warn. "This bacon is violent. Are you ok, sweetheart?"

"I'm fine. Just feeling a little off this morning…" Ellie pecks me on the lips and rests her face against my naked chest.

"Oh… Nothing a Johnson's Breakfast of Champions won't fix, hey?"

Ellie breathes deeply, stifling a hot chuckle and the hotness of her breath has my cock stirring again. He clearly hasn't had enough and waking up next to Ellie's naked body had him on high alert the second my eyes popped open.

I rarely wake up with such a jump in my step. I've put it down to getting old – the knees aren't what they used to be. I can't remember the last time I cooked fucking bacon and eggs for breakfast, let alone jolting upright in bed, ready for whatever they day brings.

That's just what this woman does to me. She's everything I've been missing in my life. Her aura in this lonely apartment has brought back the colour and sunshine. Her smiles brighten the place, lighting up the dark corners on my life like no other.

"Scrambled or fried eggs?" I place the bacon on some paper towel to allow the evil, splattering oil to soak in.

"Scrambled. Always scrambled." Ellie chimes and pulls a seat at the tiny two-seater table in the corner of the kitchen. "Wow… You're really doing your homework on this holiday." Ellie finds another stack of brochures I've been studying, and when I look over, she's plucked the Philadelphia brochure from the pile. "You could just do a massive road trip or something…"

I gulp down. The vile rising up my throat forces me to cough a spluttering gag. The force of it makes me hunch over, clutching my chest. I drop the tongs to the bench and Ellie's straight to her feet and slapping me on the back.

"Are you ok?" Ellies gasps, worry pulling her eyes.

"Yeah," I lie.

I'm not OK. One day, she's going to find out what's really going on.

I've promised myself I'm going to tell her, but I can't bring myself to do it just yet. Not after last night. Not after we've finally got rid of the giant problem that is her brother.

There's a reason I've got so many destination magazines laying around the place, but for as long as Ellie thinks I'm just planning a vacation, then I'm going to ride that wave until I can't any longer. She doesn't need to know… Not yet.

I recover from my coughing fit and we enjoy breakfast together, planning a trip in Philadelphia together. Ellie has amazing ideas, and all of her interests trump mine seven-fold. Relaxing in a day spa and enjoying a wine tasting sure as hell sounds a lot better than hiking up some random mountain for two days.

"Maybe I will hire you as my travel agent?" I say, popping the last piece of bacon into my mouth.

Ellie leans across and kisses me.

"I'd be your anything if you asked me too," Ellie says.

I smile, and when my phone pings, Ellie stands up and clears the plates.

"Shit!" I call out, looking at my phone. "Is that the time? I've got to go!"

Ellie searches for a clock on the wall, but I've never got around to putting one up. When I quickly tell her the time, she's panicked and rushes to get dressed too.

"I have to be at the coffee shop in fifteen minutes!" Ellie gasps, racing in front of me to my bedroom.

I watch her ass bounce as we jog up the hallway. With every step, her round cheeks briefly peek out from under the hockey jersey, teasing my eyes. The luscious sight of her curvy booty tingles my groin, and when she breaks into my room and removes the jersey, shaking her dark hair with a sexy, slow motion like movement, I move in behind her and press my crotch against her lacey panties.

"How quick do you think we can be?" I growl into her ear, reaching down for a handful of her rounded ass.

Ellie collapses to the bed with her hands to support her. She's bent over and my hands search her rear, grabbing and slapping with hungry desire stiffening my cock.

"Don't you have to be at training?" Ellie moans, her head bobbing between the gap between her arms.

I slap her ass gently, watching it wobble before my eyes. "Yeah… But I can be quick…"

I've never been late for training in my career. I pride myself on being a true professional. That's half the reason I'm captain of the best team in the country. I'm disciplined and every minor detail, including punctuality, matters to me.

I've also never had an ass like this to stop me from walking out the door.

I move in behind Ellie and she's shaking her ass against my pants. My cock is rock hard and when I reach down, it bursts from my pants as I drop them to my feet.

"Fuck I love this ass…" I grunt from the back of my throat.

Ellie wiggles her hips, and when she looks over her shoulder at me, her green eyes are hidden behind hooded eyelids. I feel the passion inside of her bursting out and it's like she's willing me to be late… Just for her.

This woman. This fucking woman.

My hands roam over the lacey black panties that teased me all the way back to my bedroom. Ellie's bent over, and when she reaches around, grips the waistband and slides down her own panties, I know this woman is made for me.

"Yes, baby… Show me how wet you are…"

Ellie uses her hand to spread her full, curvaceous ass before my eyes. I watch her folds open before me, and she uses a second hand to guide herself open even further.

"You're dripping for me," I grunt, moistening a finger in my mouth and sliding it against her swollen clit.

Ellie moans under my touch, and I've never wanted to hear a girl scream my name so bad. I'm a world-famous ice hockey player and I've had my share of women. Beautiful girls from all across the globe, gorgeous in their own rights.

But none of them even compare to this amazing lady.

"Ellie…" My voice softens, the growl becoming softer and more intimate as I rise to my feet and grip my cock. "I'm going to fuck you now…"

Ellie looks back at me, nodding. "Yes, baby… Please fuck me."

I chuckle a deep laugh that builds deep inside of me. Hearing her beg for it makes me love this woman even more.

Love this woman? Love? Love???!!!

My mind flashes before me. Seeing Ellie searching through the magazines, unbeknownst about what's really going on behind the scenes of my dwindling career. I still don't know what's going to happen at the end of this season, but my life in Vancouver may be coming to an end.

At least, I thought it was.

Could I leave now? That dangerous thought that just crossed my mind… Loving Ellie both excites me and scares the living shit out of me at the same time.

I love her.

I can't just leave that behind in the name of sport and money. Can I?

"Baby?" Ellie's voice catches me in a trance. I look down, my hand is still clutching her ass, and my cock is bordering the entrance to her glistening pussy. I've been so lost in thought, I'm leaving her waiting. "Is everything ok?"

"Everything's fine…" I say, gripping myself and pushing all my thoughts aside.

Whatever will be, will be. Right now, this woman needs me to fuck her. So I'm damn well going to do that.

I shuffle forward, my pants still hooked around my ankles. Gripping my cock, I nudge it between Ellie's sweet, sweet folds. She moans and once more, her head dips between her arms. I slide my cock over her clit and watch her squirm and wiggle so I'm pushing forward at her entrance.

I slide inside and the tightness of her warm, wet pussy has me gripping her curvy hips with full hands.

"Oh, yes! Fuck!" Ellie moans, her sexy voice spurring me on with hard, fast thrusts.

"Oh, take it baby… You take it so good…"

"Fuck me, Miles, baby… Fuck me just like that…"

My hand slaps her sexy ass. Ellie looks back with her bottom lip between her teeth, her eyes seductive and so fucking hot. Ellie moves her hips, shaking her ass against my body as skin-on-skin slaps and echoes around the bedroom.

Time is forgotten. We'll be late. But who gives a shit?

I push deeper inside her, letting her take my full length. Feeling her pussy tense around my cock has my belly bursting with fireworks, and I feel myself readying both our bodies for the climax.

Ellie screams out, her hair a wicked, wild mess in front of me. Her body is round and perfect for me. Her butt is shaking, every thrust of my hips sending a rippling wave right up her hips. I can't get enough of her, every part of me is in awe of how fucking sexy she is.

Gasping for breath, my cock bursts with a wave of heat, pulsing deep inside Ellie. She grips the sheets and pulls them from the bed. I feel her tightening around me, and as the raging warmth building inside of me works its way down, Ellie starts screaming with her own climax gripping my hard length deep inside her.

We're both on the edge, bordering on the world of pure satisfaction. My head is hazy, and with each deep thrust, I feel the words reach the tip of my tongue.

"Oh! Miles! There! There! There! Don't stop! OHHHH-HHHH!!!!"

Ellie collapses in front of me, and I grab her hips and pull her back against me. Her hot body tips me over the edge, and as my cock releases, so does my mind and I lose all control over my body.

"Oh! Ellie! I fucking love you!"

CHAPTER SIX

Ellie

*H*e loves me? Is that what he said? He said he loves *fucking* me... Didn't he?

I burst through the door to the coffee shop, *The Steaming Joe*. Removing my beanie and coat, I look up and Old Geoff is glaring across the counter at me. His bushy brows are raised in the same stupid way they always are...

I know the look. It means it's going to be a long fucking day.

"I'm not sure who's watch you're using, but the batteries need replacing," Old Geoff calls out, his finger tapping the silver watch on his wrist.

The coffee shop is already busy. Surprise surprise. It always is. Downtown Vancouver is a bustling business district, and for over two decades, *The Steaming Joe* has been the one stop coffee shop for suited men in the morning, tired moms during morning tea, and relaxed students seeking out a sweet treat on their way home from school.

"Sorry, Geoff," I mumble, clutching my stomach.

A queasy feeling bubbles and I'm not sure what's making me feel this way. It can't be the scrambled eggs Miles made; they were fucking delicious. I love a man who can cook, and to follow it up the way he did in the bedroom, boy, I could get used to that.

'I fucking love you…'

Miles' voice echoes through my absent mind. I grab my disgusting dark green apron and begin working the tables. My feet drag as I allow my thoughts to drift while collecting empty mugs and plates. Half-eaten muffins and the foul stench of soymilk lattes send my stomach rolling over with a horrid whirling feeling.

'I fucking love you…'

I sink into one of the booths to take a load off. Old Geoff is distracted by the increased amount of tickets for takeout coffee being thrown his way. His face is red, and his scowl is fiercer than usual, so I know I'm safe to put my feet up for at least a few peaceful minutes.

It's been a long night and I'm really not feeling too flash today.

I stare out of the window of the café and see the busy bodies of important businessmen and woman striding up the streets, all studying their watches and cell phones with hard expressions. The steaming streets are chaotic at this time of day, and I couldn't think of anything worse than joining those people on the rat race into the office.

I've never understood it. For me, work is just that… Work.

I enjoy working at *The Steaming Joe.* I've been here a few years now, and despite what Old Geoff might tell you about my work ethic, it's a fucking good job.

As I rest my head on the table, an ear-splitting bell chimes and I shoot up. Looking across behind the counter, I see my boss shaking his fist at me, waving me down.

Fuck. Busted.

With a deep sigh, I push up off the chair, collect the mugs and shoot down to the counter.

"What's up, Boss?" I chime.

Old Geoff stares at me, his grey hair extra frizzy and wiry today. "Takes these to table twenty-nine. They've been waiting far too long."

He shoves two plates of scrambled eggs and French toast in my chest. I go to grab the plates, but the force behind Old Geoff's hand sends one slice of toast falling to the floor.

"Fucking hell, Ellie!" Old Geoff screams, his face almost catching on fire he's so red.

"What? That's not my fault! If you passed them nicely-"

"Oh no… Nothing is ever your fault…"

A wafting scent of scrambled eggs floats from the plate in my hand and my stomach gives a deep hurling motion. It's like I've just zoomed down a steep hill. I force myself to gulp down, hoping to hell that it will force the vile back down.

"Geoff…"

I do my best to interrupt. Old Geoff needs to get these eggs away from me pronto. The eggy-steam is stiflingly my breathing and I'm going to fucking hurl any second now.

"… perfect Miss Ellie. Yet, whenever I look around… There you are. Sitting on your fucking ass again. Do you know how many times I should have fired you?"

"Geoff… Please…" I try to pass the plates off, but Old Geoff is off on one of his rants. He's not listening, and his hands are too busy flapping around wildly in a tantrum. I can't just force him to grab the plates, so I try another gulp down to stem the flow.

"But no… You can't do that anymore. I'm not allowed. You'll probably sue me or some shit, won't you?"

Another hurl of my stomach has vomit lodging at the base of my throat. I can't hold it in. Fuck. Everything around me is just a blur. Old Geoff's voice is fading. The heat prickling the back of my neck is stinging all the way around to my eyes, making them unfocused and blurry.

"I guess you're pleased with yourself… Now you're all shacked up with whatever that fucking hockey players name is…"

Old Geoff is just a blabbering blur now. I drop the plates to the floor and with a loud smash ringing out behind the counter, I cup my mouth, spin and race towards the bathroom with my apron flapping behind me.

I reach the door and kick it, nearly knocking a patron over in the process.

The nearest cubicle is still too far away, and by the time I'm hunched over the toilet bowl, half of my breakfast is cupped in my hand.

"Fuck…"

My voice echoes around the porcelain. Sweat forms across my brow and sends cold shivers through my entire body, making me shake with every hurl my stomach sends shooting up and out of my body.

After a few minutes of violent hurling, I finally think my body has finished punishing me for whatever horrid crime I've done to deserve this. I wipe my mouth and tread over to the sink, dabbing cold water on my face.

Old Geoff is waiting outside the bathroom after I've cleaned myself up, and beside him is the assistant manager, Julie. Both of them have their arms folded across their chests and Julie is holding a clipboard.

"Ellie?" Old Geoff says, his voice even more serious than usu-al.

It's easy to see where this is going, but to be honest, right now, I don't give a fuck if they fire me. My stomach is growling. My head is starting to pound. Perhaps they could just kill me and put me out of this misery instead?

"Can it wait? I'm really not feeling well…" I say, and I see Old Geoff roll his eyes. When Julie looks up at him, they share a look that isn't hard to read. No doubt about it - I'm fired. But they can damn well wait. "Look, whatever you're going to say is going to have to wait. I need to go home before I throw up in my hands again."

The day had started out so well.

Breakfast cooked by a smoking hot hockey player and a nice hot coffee… Followed by a hard fuck before I'm even dressed. The bright start was always going to be hard to continue with all day, so I accept my fate and grab my things and find the fastest way home.

I crash down on the sofa the minute I crawl inside my freezing cold apartment. Without bothering to switch the heater on, I clutch the blanket draped over the sofa and wrap myself up.

"Urgh…" I shiver, feeling sorry myself. "I fucking hate being sick."

My head throbs and the bright sunshine blazing through the window isn't doing me any favours. Wishing I had detoured via the kitchen for some aspirin and a bottle of cold water, I sink back into the soft pillows and hold a wrist over my forehead.

Why the hell do I feel so shit? It's a stomach bug for sure. Any minute now it'll all start coming out the other end, and dammit, I'm glad that didn't happen while I was standing holding those plates of scrambled eggs. *Yuk.* I feel a twitch in my gut at the thought of those eggs. It's a shame, because Miles made the best breakfast for me…

As the thought crosses my mind, I wonder whether it might be Miles' cooking causing my upset stomach. No… It can't be. It's not food poisoning, I've had that before and the pain in my gut then was like ten times worse than what I'm feeling right now.

Mind you, I've seen the contents of his fridge. Safe to say, he eats a lot of take out, and there isn't ever much food on the shelves of his refrigerator. Who knows how old that bacon is that he cooked.

I reach out for the remote to the TV, and when the screen flashes on, the weirdest sensation flows through my body at the image staring back at me from the screen.

"And the city of Vancouver is mourning today with the news that Miles Johnson, captain and hero of the Vancouver Vikings, has agreed personal terms with the New York Bombers and will see out his career in the USA and not his homeland, Canada."

My hands start to shake. A new twist in my gut feels different to the one I've been feeling all morning. It's like someone's kicked me and let me fall to the ground, only to kick me in the guts again.

"And that's not all, Joy… He's just found a lovely lady and here's a shot of them enjoying what might be one of Miles' last nights in Vancouver…"

An image of me and Miles on the sidewalk just outside of *The Bloody Viking* flashes on the screen. A stabbing pain digs into my gut, but I can't look away from the picture. I'm standing on my tiptoes, leaning up with my lips puckered, inches away from Miles' serious-looking face.

The newsreaders continue blabbering on, but it's all just a mess of words.

Miles hasn't ever mentioned moving to New York. I figured he would always stay right here in Canada. This is his home.

Not only that, but he just told me he loved me… Isn't that worth hanging around for?

Suddenly, my stomach isn't queasy. At least, if it is, I'm too upset to feel it.

I launch from the sofa and pace back and forth in front of the television. My hands ball and flashbacks of this morning work their way into my mind. We'd just made it. Miles and I were ready to take the next step after hiding everything for the past six months.

I do my best to block out the noise of the newsreaders. They're cracking jokes, laughing and waxing lyrical about how much of a fantastic move this would be for Miles. To finish his career off in New York City?

Apparently, that's the dream.

I pull my phone out and write a message to Miles through gritted teeth.

I need answers. And I need them now.

CHAPTER SEVEN

Miles

"Here's the Money Man," Parker Phillips shouts out across the locker room.

I roll my eyes, throwing my stick to the floor. There's a mix of jeers and cheers around the room, and until Coach Best walks in and demands the team's attention, I'm shrinking under the spotlight.

The guys have been at it all day. Despite all my efforts, the news has broken out in the locker room about my talks with other teams around the league. I've tried to keep it under wraps until I had made a decision.

And for good reason. The boys are pissed and they're letting me know it.

I haven't signed anything and already the hockey world is a crazy mess of rumours and made-up figures about my 'massive salary'.

All the offers haven't been filed yet. My agent is still talking to Boston and Washington. Toronto think they're still a chance to snag my signature, but they've got more chance of winning the Stanley Cup than they've got of me pulling on one of their jerseys.

Fucking Toronto dickheads.

"Listen up!" Coach Best slaps his hands together and glares at the team from the front of the room. "I don't know what the hell you call that out there, but you all trained like dog shit tonight."

Coach Best paces in front of us, clicking a pen in one hand while the other points at us with every word he's yelling.

"Phillips. Your passing stunk tonight. My dead grandmother can pass a puck better than you did…" Parker Phillips' smug grin is quickly wiped from his face. "Jamie. Don't laugh, you sucked, too. And don't even get me started on you, Mason."

Mason Miller nods and his youthful expression is as stiff as steel.

I yank on the tape around my gloves, pull them off, and throw them in my bag. I'm waiting for my turn. A scorching blast from Coach Best is incoming any second now. Get it over with, already. If Parker Phillips had a horrible session, then Coach is saving his best insults for me.

I couldn't keep up with the lads today… And as the news of my contract filtered around the rink between the boys, the pressure built around my body like a steam train dropping on my head.

I wanted out.

All I wanted to do was nestle in bed with Ellie. My new favourite place…

That tasty teaser before training wasn't enough. Quickies are great and all, but with Ellie, I want to take my time. I want to taste every inch of her soft skin. I want to tend to her every need and bow to her every wish or command. It doesn't matter what it is, I'd do anything for her.

Coach Best continues to scream inside the locker room, his face growing redder and redder with every ear-splitting yell he throws across at the team. His crew of coaching staff are rested back against the wall, nodding and grunting confirmations of everything our Head Coach says.

But I'm not listening.

All I can think about is the way I left things with Ellie.

My revelation that came out of nowhere rings in my ears more than Coach Best's insults. *'I fucking love you, Ellie.'* I didn't even get to see the look in her deep, intoxicating green eyes as I revealed my true feelings for the first time. I blew my load and startled her to a finish; I could tell. I've never seen a girl pull their pants up and get dressed so quickly.

She didn't even say it back…

"Now, whatever is going on in the media is out of our control. Miles isn't going anywhere right now. Nothing has been agreed-" Coach Best pins me with a look that is begging for a confirmation. I nod, confirming I'm not going anywhere. Yet. "So it's all speculation at this stage. If anyone, and I mean anyone-" He pins Jaxon King with a pointed look – he's always talking to the journos. "Says anything otherwise to the media, you'll have me to answer to. Got it?"

A grunting murmur satisfies Coach Best, and he steams ahead towards his office and slams the door shut.

Several of the boys head straight for the showers, and as they pass, a few whispered comments about me being a 'rich boy' or a 'money grabber' find their way across the room. Ignoring them, I fumble around to find my phone in my bag and when the screen shows a message from Ellie, a happy flutter makes everything OK again.

Until I open the message and read the text flashing before my eyes.

Ellie: Please tell me what I'm seeing isn't right... You're not leaving, are you?

My fist tightens around my phone.

Shit. Shit. Shit. Shit. Shit.

"Hey man," Noah stoops down on the bench beside me and I fake a crooked smile. "So, everything went alright last night then?"

It takes me a second to catch up. My head is a messy fucking hurricane with everything whizzing around in there right now.

"Yeah," I shrug. "Fine, bro."

Noah looks at me, his eyes focused intently on my face. "Listen..." He shuffles on the bench seat. "I just wanted to say thanks for giving me a heads up about you and Ellie. I really appreciate it, man."

Noah slaps me on the back, and I can only muster a tight smile. I'm gripping my phone so hard in my sweaty palms. I can't help but feel the wrong twin is sitting by my side. I want Ellie. I *need* Ellie.

"It's all good, bro," I say, doing my best to kill the conversation quickly.

Normally, I've got all the time in the world for Noah Edwards. He's a top guy, and an even better hockey player. But right now, the only Edwards I want to talk to, is freaking out about what those damned journos are saying in the tabloids.

"No, it really means a lot. A lot of guys out there wouldn't do what you did." Noah slaps me on the shoulder again. "I do have to ask though... What's with this deal? Ellie loves it in Vancouver. If you're planning to move, you need to tell her before you break her heart."

My throat pulses hard against my Adams apple.

"You don't think she would move?" I ask timidly.

Noah shakes his head and winces. "I can't see it. I mean, I could be wrong, man. But she's always said she's '*a Vancouver chick through and through*'."

A loud shout from down the hall has Noah jumping from the seat, and as he goes to move away, he looks down at me, drawing a swallowed breath.

"Just talk to her. If it's something you're seriously considering, don't beat yourself up by not talking to her about it." Noah smiles, and another scream has him wide-eyed and ready to sprint to seek out the source of the noise. "You're going to the charity dinner, right?"

I had completely forgotten about the event tomorrow night, but I nod. It's my duty as captain of the team to show up. I don't get a choice, even if I wanted one. I *have* to be there.

Noah sprints off, and the second he's out of sight, I'm changing as quickly as possible into my jeans and tee shirt. Throwing my sports bag over my shoulder, I tap out a quick message to Ellie on the way out of the locker room. I ask where she is, and when she finally replies, I'm in my car and driving towards her apartment block in heavy traffic.

It takes far too long to get there, but when I do, I see Ellie peek through the curtains of her apartment window. She buzzes me up and when I finally reach her front door, I'm panting hard.

I drum my knuckles on the wooden door, and the second I do, Ellie pulls it open.

"Sweetie…"

I lunge forward, catching Ellie in my outstretched arms. She sobs into my shoulder, and my heart aches beneath her trembling body.

She's shaking, struggling for breath and it's all my fault.

Idiot. You're a fucking idiot.

"Ellie," I pull her back and look into her blood-shot eyes. The stunning green of her gaze is overtaken by wet tears and a painful puffy redness. "Sweetheart, please… Let's sit down."

Ellie leads the way towards her living room. She's pulled the curtains shut, so the room is a soft darkness. There are three empty water bottles on the floor, and an empty packet of painkillers beside them.

"Um," I hesitate, looking around the room. "Is everything ok?" It crosses my mind that it's only three o'clock and Ellie should still be at work. I've been so swarmed with everything that time has disappeared from reality. "Why aren't you at the cafe?"

"Sick," Ellie mumbles.

"Aw, baby… Do you need anything?"

Ellie shakes her head and snuffles a loud sniff. I guide her down to the sofa and glide my hand across her back. Looking around, I see the TV still on the news channel. The scrolling text along the bottom of the screen flashes.

Squinting, I see my name written in bold, capital letters: MILES JOHNSON ON THE MOVE TO THE BIG APPLE.

"Is it true?" Ellie says, following my gaze to the screen. "Are you really moving to New York?"

My heart races and I reach across to clutch Ellie's hands. They're freezing cold. She's shaking, so I snuggle in closer and hold her tight.

"Yes… And no," I say, and Ellie looks at me with a puzzled frown. "There have been talks. I'm approaching thirty-seven years old, and my career is nearly over, babe. My agent thinks it's a good idea to try for one final big-money contract." The headlines start playing on the TV and, of course, I'm the leading news story in Vancouver today. "So, as you can see, the media is going crazy."

"You're stealing my moment…" Ellie says, a hint of her usual bright and bubbly nature seeping into her croaky voice.

"What do you mean?"

"Well, that photo of us found its way to the news, too. But all anybody cares about is that you're…" Ellie stops, and then looks to the floor. "Leaving."

I spin and drop to the floor so I'm kneeling in front of Ellie. I clutch her hands and pull them to my lips. Smothering her hands in kisses, I trail up her arms, rising to my feet as I catch her cheeks and press a deep kiss to her mouth, before dropping back to my knees and grabbing her hands once more.

"Baby, I don't know what is going to happen with these contract shenanigans," I say. "It's part of the business I'm in. One minute a big move could be on, the next, it's gone. New York could pull out tomorrow…" I point to the TV and the news anchor is chatting to the weatherman about the heatwave due this summer. "Who knows how it's going to play out… But what I do know, is that I promise to tell you every step of the way what is going on. I owe that to you."

Ellie's hands shake in mine. I grip harder and pull her gaze to mine. A tiny smile creeps at the edges of her glorious lips, sending a flutter tickling through my stomach.

"What I said this morning…" I blurt out, the words so quick they form one jumbled sentence. My heart is racing, and I need to get this off my chest quickly. "I meant them. I meant every single word." Ellie looks at me, the tiny smile growing bigger.

"Yes, Ellie. I fucking love you. And I'm just glad you're smiling... This morning, I wasn't so sure."

"Why wouldn't I smile?"

"I don't know..." I shrug. "No ones ever said those words to me before... So why would you-"

Ellie shuffles forward on the sofa and presses her finger to my lips, cutting my words in an instant.

"Miles... I love you, too."

"You do?" I say, my words muffled by Ellie's firm finger.

"I do."

"Oh. Well..." My eyes flick from side to side.

I've got no idea where to look or what to say now, but when I look back at Ellie and she's just sitting there with that special sparkle slowly returning to her eyes, I know exactly what to say.

"Baby, come with me to this Charity Gala event I have to go to tomorrow night?"

"Are you asking me to be your date to a Vikings event?" Ellie's eyes pop, and when I nod, she claps her hands in front of her chest. "Oh, yay! Hazel will be so jealous!"

Laughing, I stand up and pull Ellie with me. We kiss and only when I crunch an empty packet of painkillers with my foot does it cross my mind that Ellie is still unwell.

"So why are you home anyway? And what's with all this mess? Are you ok?"

Ellie looks down and crosses her arms across her chest. Her brows shoot up and she's popped a hip out.

"Well, Mister... I've been wanting to ask you about your bacon situation..." Ellie's eyes change to a hard glare. "I was sick at work today. A few hours after you fed me... How old was that bacon?"

I shrug, a frown pulling my face. "I only bought it a few days ago... I always cook bacon. It's a staple of any healthy man's diet."

Ellie taps her foot.

"Hmmm... I don't know what is was then. I feel OK now, though. And if I steer clear of your cooking, hopefully..." Ellie crosses her fingers and waves them in front of my face. "I can attend this charity dinner without throwing up all over the guests."

Shaking my head, I tackle Ellie to the sofa and smother her cackling laughter with a hard kiss.

CHAPTER EIGHT

Ellie

I look into the mirror and run a hand over my stomach, staring back at myself with a sideways twist. Every girl has to check how curvy their ass looks in their dress, right? Well, mine always pops. And it's fucking amazing.

Miles' instructions were simple: 'elegant, but sexy. I know you won't have any trouble with that, though.'

I've been to gala events, charity raffles and fancy functions before. But none of them have felt like this.

If what the news outlets are saying is true, this might be my only chance to stand side by side with the man I've fallen so deeply in love for. If Miles decides to deal a crushing blow to my heart, and moves cities, I'm not going to stand in his way. He's worked so fucking hard to get where he is in his career, so to have one final shot at a big contract, it's the least he deserves.

My phones buzzes on the bed, and when I open the message, an excited flutter makes my tummy turn. I think its excitement making me feel nauseous... My stomach is still feeling the effects of whatever bad bug I've eaten, but there's no fucking way I'm missing this event.

Hazel: Don't forget to send me a pic babe!

I smile and hold my phone up to take a quick selfie in the mirror to send it to my best friend.

My emerald-green gown is hugging my figure, falling just short of my knees. Black heels make my legs appear three times longer than they really are, and my hair holds curls in tight ringlets. I've spent the last hour perfecting and taming my hair, until finally I was satisfied and added silver jewellery accessories to complete my look.

Me: Wish me luck!

I hit send on the picture and Hazel helps my confidence with a prompt thumbs up reply, followed a three flame emojis. With a quick glance to my watch, I grab my sparkling silver clutch, and head downstairs.

I'm only waiting on the sidewalk for a moment before a glossy, black limousine turns the corner with a long, sweeping curve. The licence plate reads 'VIKINGS', and a smile touches my lips. I might have been around professional hockey players my entire life, but the fame and glory of it all was only ever for Noah to enjoy.

Until now.

The limo pulls up, and when it comes to a halt, Miles' handsome face pops out from the sunroof. Leaning back against the hole in the roof, he's gripping a champagne glass. Music pumps from the limo, bass making the entire stretch of the vehicle vibrate on the street.

"Well?" Miles says, his golden eyes popping. "What do you think?"

I can only see from his chest up, but the tuxedo he's wearing in one of the sexiest fucking things I've ever seen. The black suit hugs his arms, and when he curls to take a sip from the flute,

I can still see his bulging arm muscles through the perfectly tailored fabric. His sandy blonde hair is combed over, and when he smiles at me, I practically melt to the ground.

"When you said pick me up, I thought-" I stop, thinking. "Well, I didn't expect this."

"Only the best for my girl..." Miles says, blowing me a kiss. "Wait there, I'll come down."

Miles' head disappears from the sunroof, only to reappear seconds later from the door halfway down the limo. He folds out and when he's steps across to meet me, before I can even take in his tall, well-dressed handsomeness, he's dipping me into a tight, warm kiss.

"Mmmm," Miles' groans, releasing his hot lips from mine. "I've missed you today."

His golden eyes are filled with passion, and all I want to do is rip the blazer from around his shoulders a bite down on every inch of his sexy body.

"I've missed you, too," I smile, watching Miles' eyes dance around my body. "Let's get this thing over with so you can take me back to your place."

Miles runs a finger across my belly, sending warm flutters down to my core. His eyes narrow towards the whisper of cleavage my gown shows off and my body reacts instantly with a flush of goosepimples.

"Or we could just blow the whole thing off and go upstairs right now..."

"Hmmmm..." I wrap my arms around Miles' neck and lean in close to his face. "As tempting as that is, I've always wanted to ride in a limousine."

Miles smiles and presses a kiss to my forehead. He takes me by the hand and when he leads me to the open door, I get a waft of his citrusy scented cologne while checking out his tight behind. It looks extra cosy in his tight dress pants.

I slap his ass cheekily, and when he spins to hold the door, his tongue is between his teeth.

"Did you just say you've always wanted a *ride* in a limo?" Miles' eyes catch my body again.

"That's what I said," I nod, slyly grabbing a quick handful of Miles' cock before shrinking down into the flashy, luxurious cabin of the limo.

The drive to the event is hot, steamy and everything a limousine ride with a hockey player dressed in a tuxedo should be. At one point, while my lips were tightly around his round cock, Miles tapped on the window and demanded we take the long way to the function centre. It allowed me to rise up, pull my panties to the side, and get the limo ride of every girl's dream.

Finally, when the driver gives two tiny knocks on the glass, Miles peers out the dark, heavily tinted windows and turns to face me.

"We're here, baby," he says, swiping at his hair which is now ruffled and untidy.

"Sorry about your hair," I say, reaching out to guide his sandy locks back.

Miles leans in and dives his tongue deep inside my mouth, sliding an arm around my back and pulling me closer to his body. We've just finished each other, yet, everything about this man has my pussy clenching and screaming out for more.

I can't get enough.

And judging by the hardness tenting his pants - neither can Miles.

"Don't be sorry, baby…" Miles says, adjusting his large erection so it's not as obvious. "I kinda liked the way you used it as leverage."

"You're just so big," I tease. "It's not my fault I practically need a ladder to get down on you."

Miles chuckles and stares through the dark tint. I follow his gaze and shuffle across so I'm right beside him. I thread my fingers through his, sensing that he's not exactly pumped about stepping out onto the bright red carpet that's directly under the limo.

"Is everything ok?" I ask, gripping his hand tightly.

Miles sighs a resigned breath. "Yeah. It's fine. It doesn't matter how many times you do it… Sometimes, the glamour and attention feels intrusive." He turns to face me, his eyes catching mine. "But at least this time, I've got someone to show off."

My stomach flutters. The fact that I'm someone anybody wants to show off is special. I've never been that girl, despite my past relationships. I've been hidden away, outcast from family events to the point where I was completely ignored at a wedding my boyfriend at the time invited me to.

I've never let it get to me, though. I've used it to grow and motivate myself to be a confident woman who is proud of who I am. To be proud of my loud, obnoxious personality. To be proud of my body and *all* of my curves.

And today, I get to reap the rewards.

Today, I get to walk hand in hand with Vancouver's Chosen One.

"Come on," I say, squeezing Miles' hand tight. "Let's do this."

Miles presses a kiss to my lips and when a man outside the vehicle pulls the door open, Miles slides out and guides me up with him. The bright sky makes me squint, and it takes a second for my eyes to adjust.

Clicks and flashes meet my gaze when I look up. I run a hand down my dress to make damn sure it's not tucked in between my ass cheeks. What a debut on this world that would be.

I loop my arm through Miles', and he looks down at me with a bright teethy smile. He feels warm and soft by my side. Like a giant cuddly bear, I snuggle in closer, holding his thick arm with both hands.

We move towards the large entrance doors of the function centre where security is standing, guarding the entrance. There's a cool, crisp breeze floating around the air, and the buzz of excitement surrounding us is intoxicating.

The function centre is an old sandstone building on the outskirts of Vancouver. Normally the bright green lawn and perfectly hedged shrubs has children running and playing in front of the grand structure, but as I walk arm in arm with Miles up the red carpet, all I can see is a line of paparazzi roped off from us, forced to keep their distance as they snap a gazillion photos, one after the other. Blinding flash after blinding flash.

"Mr. Johnson! Mr. Johnson!"

"Miles Johnson! A moment please?"

"Miles! Sir! Miles!"

A group of short guys, each with a headset and notepad, are running along the sectioned off area, waving their arms above their heads. With a swift movement, Miles' slides my arm from his, and grabs my hand instead.

He's squeezing hard, like he's expecting something bad to happen and he needs to protect me.

My body gives a nervous shiver that rolls down my spine. My heart begins racing and I can't help but think that I'd be the worst hockey player. My nerves are shooting through my body, making me twitch and jerk with every new noise or flash I see. The rumbling in my stomach rolls over, reigniting the sick feeling I've been fighting off all day.

Oh God, don't throw up now! Not here, Ellie!

Another round of loud shouts directed at us make me cower into Miles. My belly stings with a painful lurch, forcing me to gulp down hard. Miles is standing tall and strong. He's focused, unfazed by the carnival scenes around us.

"Miles Johnson! Are you moving to New York? A nod or shake of the head will do fine, Mr Johnson…"

"New York? Over the Vikings?"

"Miles! Can we get a moment of your time?"

Sweat beads every inch of my skin, and the only thing making me feel calmer is the giant statue that is gripping my hand with an increasing amount of pressure. I look up to Miles, and without looking at me, he smiles and winks.

My heart pounds inside my chest. I know I loved this man already… But watching him so calm and composed has made me fall even deeper in love with him.

How could I not?

The way he's holding me, it's like I'm the last petal on the final flower of the season. It's his duty to protect me. He's shielding me. Guarding me. And finally, when we reach the four steps leading to the doors, he turns to face me.

Miles stands in front of me, and the cameras flash wildly in his face. We're standing on the top step, like we're on display for the world to see.

Bright lights flicker and move to the music bouncing around the red carpet. I look up into Miles' eyes and he smiles softly, just like he always did when he looks at me. Without a word, he leans down and applies the deepest, most loving kiss I've ever received.

The cameras go wild. Clicks and shutters closing, all vying to get the best image of Miles Johnson and *his girl.*

He can't leave. Not now. I'm in too deep. *We're* in too deep.

CHAPTER NINE

Miles

"T hank you all for attending tonight's function. The new children's hospital will forever be grateful for the donations and support offered by all of our guests tonight."

The MC, a local radio celebrity, wraps the auction up at the front of the room. A polite applause filters around the room.

A dozen large round tables are set out in a large hall, all dressed like we're attending some fancy award ceremony.

I'm surrounded by my teammates and their dates at a table towards the back of the room. It seats twelve of us comfortably, even if half of us are huge hockey players with broader shoulders than the other men in the room.

Empty beer bottles and wine glasses scatter the table. Our plates are being cleared after a delicious meal. A collection of waitresses dressed in neat attire begin clearing a section of the dining room for a makeshift dance floor, and a DJ booth is rolled out from one side.

I pull Ellie's hand in mine and lean across to whisper in her ear.

"You know… If we left now, no one would notice."

Ellie flashes a cute smile, and I see her consider it for a moment. She looks fucking beautiful tonight. The other women in the room all look fantastic, but they're nothing compared to the stunner sitting by my side.

I know Ellie's lapping up every second of this. An event like this for a lifetime hockey fan is the ultimate dream.

She started out nervously. I don't blame her. Those freaks outside are enough to frighten the living daylights out of anyone. But the moment we stepped inside – away from the nagging and spying eyes of the media – she's embraced the magical evening.

"Can't we enjoy one dance first?" Ellie says, her green eyes gorgeous in the dimmed light.

"Of course, baby," I say, softly. My fingers fiddling with her hanging silver earrings as they flicker in the light. "We'll leave whenever you're ready." I look down at her plate and notice she's hardly touched her food. "Are you going to eat something, sweetheart? You shouldn't drink on an empty stomach."

Ellie looks at her loaded plate. A seared eye-fillet steak, charred to perfection, remains glistening in golden, melted butter. A side of vegetables has been poked and prodded by her fork, but everything else remains untouched.

"I can't eat," Ellie says, and when I pin her a stern look, she flaps a hand against my chest. "It's ok, Miles. I've only had half a glass of wine." She holds her hand against her stomach and blows out her cheeks. "And that's not sitting too well either."

"Are you sure you don't want to get out of here?" I ask, sliding my hand across her thigh. "I'll take you home and you can rest."

Ellie shakes her head and leans across for a kiss. "Baby… I think we both know if we go home, we won't be resting…"

I feel the eyes of the table staring into the side of my head. Maybe we're not talking as quietly as I thought we were.

"You're right," I whisper, my breath tickling Ellie's ear. "We might not even make it out of the limo."

Ellie giggles and the DJ starts playing the first song. A collection of hotshot football players from Texas start dancing as if they own the place.

Fucking football players.

Noah is directly across from us, and I swear he's smiling at the sight of his sister nestled in my arms. He's sitting beside Parker Phillips, who's happily chatting with his new roommate. Parker hasn't taken his eyes off her all night, and I don't think he can believe his luck at finding a new, *female* flatmate.

Mason and Jacob are here, busying themselves in a drinking contest that won't go down well with Coach Best if he finds out about it. They're keeping a peeled eye on all the talent here, seeking out their lady of the night.

Ellie rests her head on my shoulder as we watch the dancefloor fill up quickly. Curling my arm around her, I'm pulled from the moment by a pointed tap on my shoulder. I look up, and tiny beady eyes peering through glasses stare into me.

"Hello there, Miles," the man says. I recognise him from the hockey league events I've attended. "Jeff Rowlands, manager of North Carolina's up and coming hockey franchise. We met in New York a few months back..."

He stretches his hand out, and when I give a firm shake, I see Ellie twist in her seat beside me. She leans forward on the table, and though she's not looking at the man, I know she's hooked on every word he's saying.

"Yes, I remember." I look to Ellie and slide my hand back to her thigh, trying to reassure her with a gentle squeeze.

"Yes, well. Lovely event, isn't it?" Jeff looks around the room, and when I hum an uninterested response, he shakes his head, and his glasses slide down his nose. "Anyway, listen. I thought while I was in Vancouver, I would pay you a visit. I've heard the rumours and seen the news… I know you're seeking a new venture. I thought perhaps North Carolina would be the perfect place for you."

My chest tightens. Ellie's face has gone as white as the ice of Viking Arena. I can barely see her eyes, but I'm sure they're welling up at the words she's hearing. Her shoulders slump over, and I can feel her chest is heaving like she's struggling to hold it together.

I know she doesn't want this move. She's made that much clear. *Maybe she can join me?* She can come and we can start a new life together. It's a new beginning for both of us…

She'll go for that, won't she? We'd still be together, after all.

No… No, I can't do it. I can't drag her away from her home. Like Noah said, she's a Vancouver girl. I can't rip that away from her.

"We can build the team around you…" Jeff continues talking, and although I'm nodding along, all I'm thinking about is Ellie.

She's everything to me. This has been the best night I've had in a long time.

Well, nothing is forcing me to leave. I could stay… For her.

As the thought of staying in Vancouver for Ellie crosses my mind for the first time, she coughs and grabs her mouth. A combination of weird noises rumble from deep in her belly, and she quickly shoots up from her chair. She's clutching her mouth and her stomach at the same time.

I reach out to stop her but it's too late.

Ellie's face is pale. Really fucking pale. I'm stuck between the table and fucking Jeff Rowlands, and I try to stop Ellie so I can help. Reaching out, Ellie slaps my hand away and rushes from her chair. She races across the room, storming through the crowd, still clutching her mouth.

A stabbing pain hits me right in the chest. Why did she do that? She needs me. I want to help her.

Fucking Jeff, get out of the way!

"Listen, Jeff…"

I want this conversation to cease immediately. I'm not sure if Ellie's crying or what's going on, but Noah's glaring across at me. All I want to do is chase after his sister and the way he's glaring at me; he expects that as well.

Heck, I expect it of myself.

"If you want to talk to me, you need to arrange something with my agent, Jeff." I jump from my chair and look out across the room. "Right now, I need to find my girl."

I shove past Jeff and steam across the room, dodging bodies and the dozens of people vying for my attention. The footballers shout taunts from the dancefloor… Something about they do it better down south, and there's an uninviting offer to join them in a town that I've never heard of.

I don't care. There's only one thing on my mind. I can't let Ellie go. I need her in my life. Forever.

I'm not going anywhere. If Ellie is Vancouver, then so am I.

But first, I need to find her.

CHAPTER TEN

Ellie

I'm speeding across the room, holding the vile in my mouth as I push past what feels like hundreds of bodies. They're all dressed perfectly, laughing and dancing and having a fan-fuck-ing-tastic time.

And here I am, racing towards the bathroom with burning, acidic vomit lodged somewhere between my throat and my mouth, choking me with every lunging stride I take.

Vomit stains clothing, right?

That's all I can think about. A random guy in a navy-blue suit waves his arms in front of me and I'm forced to swipe at his face. "Move!" I manage to scream through a disgusting mouthful of spew.

His face scrunches and the lady's restroom is finally in view. I force the door open and ignore the three young girls who are acting sheepish in front of the mirrors. They all snap their necks as soon as the door smashes back against the wall, alerting them to my presence. A phone is rested against the mirror, the camera showing off the three girls on the screen.

I get it... Tiktok is fantastic. I'm all for dancing like a dick for the entire world to see, but right now...

"Get out! Get out!"

I force my way forward, and the girls screw their faces and quickly disappear. I collapse in front of the toilet bowl and send wave after wave of vomit splashing around the bowl. My body shivers on the cold tiles. My skin feels steaming hot. Sweat is dripping down my back. And when my stomach finally settles, I rest back against the cubicle wall, struggling to breathe.

"Fuck," I groan, swiping my wrist against the sweat on my brow. "Fuck, fuck, fuck, fuck, fuck!"

The bathroom is silent. The young girls are gone. Thank fuck for that, no one should have to witness the noise of me throwing up. Believe me.

Cold air prickles my skin and slowly, my stomach releases the cramp that has been holding on so tightly.

Fuck. I… I can't be…

My breathing isn't slowing. A gut-wrenching thought crosses my mind. It's not the first time, and the sense that I might be right is growing stronger.

I've been ill before, but not like this.

That doesn't mean you're… No. I'm not. I'd know by now…

My chest is rising and falling rapidly as I catch my breath. A rhythmic dripping noise comes from the basin and breaks the silence. It feels more like torture with every drop that echoes in the silence of my racing head.

I stare down at my purse.

I need to know. I was going to wait until after tonight. But it can't wait any longer.

My body doesn't react like this to anything. I don't get stomach cramps. It's not period pain. This isn't a bug. It's not food poisoning.

No. I know what this is.

Plus, I need to pee. So, what the hell…

I unbuckle my purse and pull the box out. Opening it quickly, I retrieve the stick and take a long, deep breath. I position myself on the toilet and relieve myself as normal, only this time, I'm holding a tiny, life-changing stick in the steady hot stream tinkling the toilet bowl.

I'm doing the math in my head. Miles is the only guy I've been with for the past six months, so that part is easy. The other night was too soon, though. Wasn't it? Can you fall pregnant that quickly? Would I be feeling the effects already?

No. I know exactly when it was.

An image of Miles flashes before my eyes. One hot, steamy passionate night of sex was the moment. There was wine. Lots of wine. We'd been getting along so well. This was all before the pressure of coming clean to Noah had buried Miles' feelings for me.

Shit.

How the hell is he going to react? He's looking to sign the last contract of his career, he's already under so much pressure. Do I need to tell him? Does he even want children?

Oh, God… I've really fucked up this time.

The stick rests on the box and as I yank my panties up and flap my dress out, I hear the squeak of the bathroom door open.

"Ellie? Ellie!"

"Miles?"

My stomach drops and I fumble to collect the pregnancy test from the floor. My cheeks flush and I spin to hide the stick and box on top of the toilet.

"Are you ok, baby? Do you need water or some crushed ice?"

Smiling, my heart leaps. *This man.* Fucking hell, if only he knew what was really going on in here, would he be so sweet and supportive?

I open the cubicle door and as I do, Miles is pacing. He has one hand scratching the back of his neck, the other fidgeting in his pocket. He's stepping quickly, panic clearly straining his eyes. When I step out, he quickly jumps across and wraps his big arms around me.

"Oh, baby… Are you ok?"

Miles' embrace is everything to me right now. He's strong and caring. He's the rock I need to get through this. My body reacts to his like we're meant to be.

We are meant to be.

But what if he wants his big move? The new contract. Big money. A team built around him, just like that dude was saying right before I nearly threw up in his lap.

This will ruin everything for Miles.

"Um, Ellie?" Miles' voice is deep. He grips my shoulders and forces our eyes to lock. "Is that… Is that… Yours?"

Miles glances over my shoulder, lifting his chin at the sight behind me. *Fuck.* A buzzing bundle of nerves makes my stomach queasy again. My hands grip on his shirt and I never want to let go. Miles has become everything to me, but any second now, once I reveal what's going on… He'll be gone.

I've never felt so small.

I gulp down. This is it.

"Yes, it's mine," I say quietly.

I look up, expecting a shocked mouth and lost eyes. Only, when I look into Miles' gorgeous golden eyes, he's not frowning. There's no confusion. His face hasn't lost all colour.

No.

He's… He's… Smiling.

"And what have you got it for?" Miles says, a strange hint of hope and optimism lifting his voice.

My heart is racing. "Well, I haven't been feeling too well… As you know. So, I bought it this afternoon before you picked me up."

Miles grunts and nods. Our bodies are close. The slight distance between us is closed off by Miles' arms, as he holds my shoulders and smiles down at me with a twinkle like I've never seen on him before.

"Have you looked? Tell me… Are you… Are you-"

"I haven't looked…" I cut Miles off, unable to stop the smile forming on my lips.

I can't believe he's reacting like this. I did not expect a giant hockey player to get so swoony over a possible surprise pregnancy. Has he forgotten this could potentially change everything *forever?* A child being born is no small thing. Our lives will never be the same.

"Is it ready?" Miles says, his eyes unmoved from the box on the toilet.

"I think so," I shrug. I spin around and Miles' hands slide between my arms and curl around my belly. He cuddles me from behind and his chin rests on top of my shoulder, his breath hot against my neck.

Unable to wipe the smile from my face, I notice his palms feel hot around my stomach. Inside my body, could be the seed of our raging passion. An excited flutter fills me, and when Miles starts rubbing my belly ever so gently, I swear I feel his breath choke.

"Baby… Would you like to look together?"

Miles hums a confirmation, and we step forward into the cubicle together. His arms remain locked around me, holding my stomach with soft hands. I reach down and collect the stick, careful not to look at the tiny window.

I spin and face Miles as he releases his hold from around me. Puffing my cheeks, I ask, "Ready?"

"Yep," Miles nods. "No! Wait!"

Miles' eyes pop wide, and as they do, his hands clasp my cheeks. He lowers down and pulls me into a deep, tender kiss. My tongue swipes across his, slowly and tentatively. It's a kiss like we've never shared before. It's not hot and steamy, bursting with lust. No. It's deep, loving and with every lather of his mouth against mine, I know this man is in it for the long haul. He loves me and I love him, no matter what the test says… He'll be by my side for the rest of our lives.

Miles pulls away. "OK. Now we're ready."

With a nervous giggle, I nod and look down.

Two lines.

Miles looks up at me, happiness oozing from the corners of his eyes in the shape of tiny tears.

"Pregnant! We're pregnant!"

CHAPTER ELEVEN

Miles

I signed my first professional contract when I was fourteen. To this day, I've always said that was the happiest day of my life. It trumped skating on the Viking Arena for the first time. It beat my debut for the Vikings. MVPs… Stanley Cup victories.

Becoming a pro hockey player was my greatest achievement. Until now.

"Baby!" I wrap Ellie in my arms and spin her around. "We're having a baby!"

Ellie's laugh fills the bathroom. It sounds like a songbird singing softly in the forest and relief floods through me. I was worried I had fucked this all up. Ellie dashed off without me, all the talk of me moving cities had become too much and she was done.

Instead, this. This!

"Miles! Miles!" Ellie shrieks as I spin her around again. "Put me down or I might throw up again! And I think you might be squeezing the baby!"

I drop Ellie to her feet and instantly fall to my knees. My hands clasp her belly and I'm kissing Ellie's stomach through the fabric of her dress.

"Oh, sorry, bubba… Daddy's sorry…"

I feel Ellie's fingers threading my hair and, in this moment, I've never been happier.

Who would have thought a dingy, run down ladies bathroom could be the host of the happiest moment of your life?

With a firm kiss to her stomach, I rise to my feet and pull Ellie in for another kiss. I can barely control my emotions. Happiness. Excitement. Jubilation. All taking over and sending adrenaline rushing through my veins.

I want to climb a fucking mountain and shout out at the world. I want to bang my chest like a god damned cave man. I'm going to be a father. Holy shit!

"You beautiful, beautiful girl," I say, smothering Ellie's mouth with another kiss. "Thank you. Thank you so much."

Ellie's eyes pop and they're the most stunning set of eyes I've ever seen. I hope my child has their mother's eyes. I hope they're every bit like their mother, their looks, personality, the works. She's the best damn human being in the world.

"Stop, Miles!" Ellie cackles, pushing me back. I force myself to let go, and beam like a goof at her. "Come on, let's get out of here. The smell of this bathroom is making me want to hurl again."

I link my hand in Ellie's and lead her out of the bathroom. In amongst the excitement of the past few minutes, I had completely forgotten about the event taking place on the other side of the wall.

The music is still pumping, and guests of the event are in the groove, dancing and jiving with each other on the dancefloor. I lead Ellie across the room with a new skip in my step. I keep her close so I can protect her body from drunken footballers or their dolled-up girlfriends.

"I just have to say goodbye to the guys, and I can meet you out the front?" I say, turning to Ellie who is busy watching Parker Phillips dance with his new roommate.

"No, I'll stay with you."

I grab Ellie by the hand and wave to a few of the guys on the dancefloor. When I glance over to the table, Noah is the only person left sitting there. He's chatting with Jeff, and they look deep in conversation. Ellie notices the man, and I see her expression drop at the sight of the newest agent trying to get me to sign up for his team.

I grip her hand firmly and steam across to slap Noah on the shoulder.

"We're getting out of here," I say, ignoring Jeff's popping eyes.

Noah looks Ellie up and down, and then glances at me. His brows crease and fuck me if that whole twin-mind-reading thing isn't real. Noah's face scrunches and a sinking feeling pulls me down.

"Is everything ok, Ellie?" Noah growls, side eyeing me.

Parker Phillips flies behind us, followed by his roommate who's giggling wildly. A loud cheer screams from the dancefloor and I just want to get the hell out of here.

"Yeah, everything's fine," Ellie says, clutching my shoulder. "Everything is absolutely perfect."

Noah grunts and his scowl isn't fading. "You're weird tonight, you know that?"

Noah pins Ellie with a look that only she would understand. Ellie shrugs and yanks on my arm so I'm left flapping a distant wave to Jeff.

After a few minutes of waiting, we flop into the limo. Ellie stares out of the window and I'm left gaping across at the majestic beauty of this woman. A few short hours ago, I was just excited to spend the night with her.

Now, knowing she's growing my baby inside of her, I'm excited to spend the rest of my life, not only with her, but with my child, too.

"Ellie, sweetheart…" I grip her thigh and she threads her fingers between mine and flashes a smile. "I want you to know… I'll be here for everything."

She smiles, but it's a smile that tells me she already knows what I'm about to say. At least, she thinks she does.

"I know, babe…" Ellie says, but when I slide down the seat so I'm on my knees below her, her attention is caught in a way it wasn't before. "Wh- what are you doing?"

My body starts to shake. I haven't planned this. Heck, I haven't planned *any* of this.

Never in a million years did I think I would wind up dating Ellie Edwards. In my head, she was never going to be interested in me. Not once did I think I would get to sleep with her. Even after that, the issue of her being Noah's sister? That was an obstacle I was sure I would never get over.

Now, having her as my girlfriend and her pregnant with my baby…

I don't need to plan anything. Life has already planned it out for me. I just need to live it.

"Ellie…" My voice is shaky, and I force myself to hold it together. "I'm not going anywhere. Forget the contracts. Forget New York. Forget fucking Jeff Rowlands." Ellie sniggers behind a hardened expression. "My point is… Right now, you're my life. Wherever you are, that's where I want to be."

"Baby… What about your career? We can come with you. The baby and me."

"The Vikings will keep me on. I can finish my career here. With you." I reach out and rub Ellie's belly. "With us."

Ellie's lips curl into a cute smile.

"And to prove this to you," I let go of Ellie's hand and dive into my pocket for my keys.

I pull the keyring from my pocket, and I can feel Ellie's eyes on the top of my head. It feels like I'm taking a penalty shot, and the entire stadium is glued to my every move. My sweaty fingers twist the key from the ring, and I shove it back in my pocket. I told you I didn't plan this, so a makeshift engagement ring by the way of a keyring will have to do for now.

Smiling, I look up at Ellie who now has her hands clasped over her mouth.

"Ellie, this might be soon. But from the moment you kissed me I knew you were the one. My heart hasn't been the same since and it only continues to grow fonder and fonder of you with every moment I spent in your presence." Ellie chokes on her breath and tears stream down her blushing cheeks. "Ellie, will you marry me?"

"Yes!" Ellie cries, throwing her arms around me. "Yes of course I will!"

I pull her into a deep embrace and her warmth and energy surrounds me in a way that fills me with the knowledge that I'm going to be a happy, happy man for the rest of my life.

EPILOGUE

Ellie

THREE YEARS LATER

"You look beautiful, babe…" Hazel says, her eyes bright. Noah clears his throat from beside us and Hazel spins and rolls her eyes at him. "Yes, darling… You look good, too. Nice touch with the pink tie, by the way."

Hazel winks at me and I can't help but beam.

Minutes from now, I'll be walking down the aisle, arm in arm with my twin brother as he gives me away to his best friend. Not only has he agreed to be a 'bridesmaid' for me, but Noah has been a rock for the past year, ever since Dad passed away.

"Red would have been better you know? Everyone knows red is the best colour," Noah grunts, tugging at his soft pink tie. "I think the Viking's would have sponsored the dress if you went with red… Not that you and money bags need the money anyway…"

Rolling my eyes, I slap Noah's shoulder and glance up at the clock.

It's time.

Actually, it's well past time. Miles would be standing up there in a nervous pile of sweat, pacing back and forth like he does when he's nervous. And that's exactly how I had planned it. The bride's allowed to be late, right?

I've done my sweating and painful wait. Thirteen hours of labour is what it took to get our feisty little bundle of joy into this wonderful world. And I don't regret a single second of the thirteen-hour process.

OK, I'm lying. It fucking sucked.

But I would do it all over again because now we've got the sassiest little girl.

"Are you ready, sweetheart?" I drop down to Lucy's level and see her eyes a clear reflection of mine. "Time to go and see Daddy."

Lucy bounces on the spot, her blonde hair perfectly straight for her parents' big day.

"Yay! Daddy! Daddy! Daddy!"

Lucy is a Daddy's girl through and through. It's no wonder. Miles *adores* her. All she has to do is look at him and he melts. It's a privilege to watch them grow with each other, both learning as much as the other, but every now and then, would it be a crime to let Mummy in? I'm the one who spent thirteen hours pushing her out for God's sake!

"Yes, yes… Daddy…" I roll my eyes and Hazel chuckles while pulling Noah along behind her.

We reach the door of the bride's suite, and when Lucy yanks it open, my feet are glued to the floor. Nerves pin me to the ground and suddenly, I'm a statue.

I've been waiting for this moment my entire life, and now that it's here, I can't believe it.

I look around.

It's just how I imagined it. Miles had made damn sure of that. Whatever I wanted, I got. My dream wedding. Right down to the tiny people on top of the cake, *hand-crafted* to look exactly like us.

Hazel slides up beside me and links her arm through mine. Her crystal blue eyes shimmer and I swear she's crying already.

"Come on. You're ready for this," Hazel says.

She gives a tug of my arm and when I step out of the doorway, I see Lucy is already walking up the aisle at the end of the corridor, her flower basket dangling on her forearm as she throws petals down the aisle quickly and runs out of sight, assumedly into Miles' arms.

"Yeah, come on, sookielala," Noah barges past, still fiddling with his tie. Music begins playing and my brother is right when he chuffs, "It's showtime."

"Stop playing with that!" Hazel smacks his hand, and he mocks an upset face. "I'm tired of telling you!"

Noah frowns with wide eyes. "Don't even think about treating your husband like she does."

He steams off, leaving Hazel and me laughing. He's only joking, of course. Hazel and Noah are the perfect married couple. And the growing pop in Hazel's belly is making Lucy incredibly excited for her first little cousin.

We follow Noah up the hall, and he joins up with the other guys who all poke and pull at his tie, sending Hazel's hands into tight fists. They make fun of Noah for having to stand on the 'girls side', but I don't care.

He's my brother. And although he might be Miles' best friend, he was mine first.

Noah links arms with Miles' brother, a kind guy from down south. They act romantic and chuckle as they break through the doorway, gasps and giggles replacing the '*naw*' noises that Lucy received.

The guests in the other room are met with the site of Hazel and an old friend of Miles' from London. There are some special guests at this wedding, but James Hawkes, a famous soccer player from Hampstead FC might just be the cream on the cake.

And then, I'm alone.

I draw a deep breath. In my head, I can hear my wedding planner screaming the countdown at me.

"*Wait for the beat to die down and then take your steps...*"

My palms are sweaty and all I can hear in the pounding of my heart in my chest. Is everyone this nervous before they walk down the aisle?

I should be excited. I *am* excited. I can't wait to be Mrs. Johnson. We have a great family already, now I want my husband, too.

Then I hear it.

"The beat has stopped..." I mumble, and as I do, I grip my flowers against my chest and step forward.

It's magical. White roses lines the aisle in tall vases. The white carpet is leading the way to a raised platform. When I look up, all I can see is Miles. There are several people gathered around him. His brothers. His friends. My brother. My friends.

But all I see is... Miles.

Sandy blonde hair. A rough stubble that he insisted looks good, and dammit, he's right. The crisp white suit is the perfect choice. His round shoulders are still broad and solid, even though he's no longer playing with the team anymore.

Miles flashes a smile and quickly wipes at the corner of his eye. Lucy is standing in front of him, griping her tiny bouquet of flowers so tightly. They look so much alike. The same hair. The same smile. The same loving gaze directed at me.

How did I get so lucky?

I step up the raised platform and meet Miles with a wide grin. His cheeks are flushed red, his eyes glistening in the moisture of his tears. We're close. So close Miles leans in, and for a moment, I think he's about to kiss me.

I jolt back, my eyes popping with shock.

"You can't kiss me before he says you can!" I pin the celebrant who's just staring at me blankly. "It's bad luck!"

Miles smiles and shakes his head. "Ah, baby… I was just going to tell you how beautiful you look…"

"Oh…" I mumble, my eyes shifting.

There's a giggle around the room and for a moment I feel like I'm the star hockey player on the ice. I'm the centre of attention and the star of the team. I guess, in a way, I am. At least for today. Then Miles can go back to being Vancouvers favourite legend. The city is sold on the fact that he chose to stay and sign on for one more year because he loved the Vikings so much. And that's fine. They can think that.

But I know Miles Johnson stayed for me. He stayed for his daughter. Most of all, he stayed for his family.

"Miles Johnson, do you take Ellie Edwards to be your lawfully wedded wife?"

"I do," Miles confirms.

"Ellie," The celebrant twists and faces me. I take a breath and do my best not to wipe the hot tear rolling down my cheek. "Do you take this man, Miles Johnson, to be your lawfully wedded husband?"

"I do."

"It is with great pleasure that I now announce you husband and wife. Miles… Now…" The celebrant leans in close, eyeballs Miles before looking at me with a cheeky grin. "Now, you may now kiss the bride."

Miles beams and presses his lips to mine. His hands pull me in closer and closer, but it's still not enough. It never will be enough. I can't have too much of this man, and now that he's mine forever, I don't need anything else.

- THE END –

****

Thank you so much for reading CAPTAIN'S CURVY PUCK! **This was Miles and Ellie's story - I hope you enjoyed the second book in the series.**

For a FREE preview of Faye and Parker's story in Book Three – Puck My Roommate, keep reading!

Excerpt from Next In Series

Puck My Roommate - Book Three - The Locker Room Series

CHAPTER ONE

Parker Phillips

My hands grip the stick, my heart sending pulses around my body like a ticking time bomb. I glance to the clock. Only thirty seconds to go.

We've done it again.

Boston is supposed to be good at hockey, right?

Well, they're no match for us. Eight to zero. EIGHT. Eight fucking goals to none.

The Vancouver Vikings are having the season of a lifetime. I'm a big part of that. This is my breakout season. I've worked fucking hard to get here, and as I pass the puck sideways to Noah Edwards, our star MVP, I can't help but glow with the feeling of finally making it as a professional hockey player.

My place on the ice has been solid this season. I've been at the Vikings a few years now, but with the talent in our locker room, it hasn't been easy make regular appearances.

"Parker! Move your ass!" Miles Johnson, my captain and pain in my ass, screams from behind me. "We haven't won anything yet!"

The clock is about to call time, and even though it's another demolition in the bag, the reason we're at this level is because Miles doesn't release the pressure. His intensity is insane. Relentless. There is no rest until the final buzzer sounds.

This is the bigtime.

National Hockey League.

Where every game counts. Every *second* of every game counts.

And when you play in Vancouver - you're never allowed to forget it.

Rolling my eyes, I shift towards the opposition player in front of me. He shields the puck. Lifting my stick, I poke and prod, careful not to give away the foul. The crowd is chanting down the final seconds, and when the buzzer final echoes around the arena, I pump my fist in the air.

"And that's game!"

A loud roar rattles the roof of the Viking Arena. Fans stand on their seats, waving scarfs and banners in a deep sea of red. I can't help but smile. The feeling of belonging rumbles in my chest and I raise a hand to accept the ovation.

This is my life. Hockey and Vikings. Nothing else matters.

The sorry-looking Boston players skate off the ice. Their helmets in their hands and their heads bowed. They're just the latest victims of a team who is on track to smash the record books. My Viking teammates gather in the centre of the rink, raising our hands as a team, applauding the crowd. We show our appreciation for their support, without them, we wouldn't be half the team we are.

Coach Best rounds us in, and when Jacob Rule skates past me, his boyish grin wider than ever, I follow in behind towards the locker room.

When I step inside the large red door of the locker room, it's a mix of guttural roars from the players, excited hugs and kisses from family and friends, and drenching Gatorade, splashing around the room as the boys celebrate.

"Fucking boys! Top win tonight, fellas! Top win!"

"On point, boys!"

"Another one in the bag!"

A wide smile stretches my lips as I move over to my locker. Jamie Fisher jumps in a circle, splashing red sports drink around the room like he's standing on an F1 podium, spraying champagne. Jacob Rule joins in and they drown Miles by holding two bottles over his head, covering him in the sticky, sugary refreshment.

"Alright, alright, alright..." Coach Best smacks his hands together and instantly he has the attention of the room. "Good win tonight. We're not to get carried away though. Stay focused. We have another game in two days. They're coming thick and fast now. So don't do anything stupid." He pins Jacob with a stern look. "And that includes you, dipshit."

Jacob holds his hands up in innocence as Coach Best disappears from the room. He has media commitments and he's dragged Noah away with him for the post-game interview.

I slump down on the bench seat and rest my head against the locker. Looking across the room, Aiden is with his sister. His parents are making their way across to Miles, who is leaning up against the wall. He yanks his gloves off as he chats with Ellie Edwards, and when Aiden's parents nudge him, he shakes their hands.

Ellie moves in and smiles. She's a superfan if I've ever seen one, and she's always got Miles' back. It's a cute story how her and Miles got together... I've never been in love, but if I ever do fall for someone, I hope my love is as strong as theirs.

"What the fuck was up with you tonight, cockface?" Jacob Rule drops the empty bottle of red Gatorade and sinks in beside me, his bulky body making the bench seat dip. "You played like shit."

"Fuck off I did..." I grunt, brows narrowing at Jacob. "How many shots did you shoot wide?"

Jacob's one of the younger guys on the team. He's a big boy, even taller than my six-foot-eight frame. He knows how to throw his weight around, but at the same time, his tongue does a good job of getting him into trouble on the ice.

"It's that new roommate of yours, isn't it?" Jacob pokes his tongue in the side of his cheek, and I want to fucking punch it. "She's getting to you. What's her name again… Fiona?"

"It's *Faye*."

A weird bubbling in my tummy rumbles when I say her name. She's only been in my life for a few days, but every time I think about her my body does this weird tummy flip thing that makes me feel like I've just raced down a steep hill.

"Faye! That's it!" Jacob slaps his knee. "And where is the stunner tonight?"

I spin and pin Jacob with a hard look. "You probably scared her off. Now fuck off to the showers, would you? You're stinking the place out."

Jacob giggles that stupid boyish laugh that I hate and finally, he disappears. With a groan, I rip my jersey off and throw it in my sports bag.

Now all I can think about now is Faye. *God dammit.* Just as I've been able to remove her from the front of my mind, she's back again.

She's my new roommate. *Faye Franklin.* I haven't seen too much of her, with training and the lead up to the game this week. From what I have seen, the blonde beauty from the States is everything I didn't expect when I put the call out for a flatmate.

The tummy-flip is back when I picture her blonde hair. The way she swished and twirled it around her fingers as she stooped over the cooktop this morning, baking those delicate French cookies. I did my best to control my eyes - she's my new roommate after all.

Scoping out her extra curvy hips and plump backside is off-limits, right?

That breaks some sort of 'roommate code' or something, surely...

I couldn't help myself. I love a woman with curves. And Faye has plenty. Her chest pops with a bust that makes me want to smother my face in-between her smooth tits. It's the way she throws her hair over her shoulder as she speaks... The way she swings the tongs over her delicately painted fingernails while she waits for the over to bing…

And then there's her eyes… Those magical, intoxicating, dreamy green eyes.

I've never had a roommate. I'm 34 years old. Lucky for me, money has never been a problem so I never felt the need for one.

The only reason I put the ad for a roommate was for the companionship I thought having another dude around might bring. A big old luxury apartment is great and all, but with two vacant bedrooms and an enormous living quarters for one person… The fancy ducted heating isn't enough to shift the cold, loneliness of a vacant apartment.

Faye Franklin put her application up within minutes of me posting the ad. Her smiling picture flashed up on my phone and I couldn't hit dial quick enough.

The best part is, she's not even into hockey. Not that I know of, anyway. We haven't had the time to chat properly.

"Hey man." Noah Edwards crosses his arms in front of me and I notice he's showered and already dressed. *How long have I been sitting here thinking about Faye?* "You heading out tonight?"

"Nah," I say, lifting my shoulders with a lazy shrug. "I'd better get home."

"Yeah! So you can whisper sweet nothings in Fiona's ear!"

Jacob's voice circles around Noah and when I look over at him, he's running a comb through his matted wet hair. His face is alive with amusement. He thinks he's fucking hilarious and my fingers curl at the sight of the fucking grin he's wearing.

"It's Faye, dickhead! Faye!"

"Faye? *Faye-king* that she's interested in you so she can trash that shit apartment and take your flatscreen!" Jacob chuckles. He's searching for a high five, but Noah just stares at him with a blank face. Jacob throws his head back with laughter anyway, and leaves.

I breathe a deep sigh and rolls my eyes at Noah who's still standing in front of me.

"New roommate?" Noah asks, and I confirm with a nod. "What's going on there? It's about time you paired up, man."

"Ha! Nah, bro. It's not like that. I don't see her that way…"

Liar.

"Well, if you two get bored later, come down to The Bloody Viking. All the boys are going. Damn good win tonight. We should celebrate."

I nod and Noah grips his sports bag and loops it over his shoulder. I lean back and watch as he leaves the locker room, wondering what he meant by 'about time I paired up'.

Thirty-four isn't old, is it? Is there a time frame for these things?

I know I'm not getting any younger but I've never even thought about getting a girlfriend. My head had always been focused on hockey. Hockey, hockey, hockey and more hockey. I've been working so hard to get in the team, and finally this season, my hard work has paid off.

Throwing all that away for a shot at love is crazy man's talk.

Not for Faye it's not.

I shake my head. It's an attempt to rid her from my mind, but it doesn't work.

She's all I can think about, so the only way to stop that is find her as quickly as possible, look her deep in those gorgeous green eyes of hers and prove to myself that she's not worth throwing all my hard work away for.

That should work, right?

Buy this book at your favorite paperback store or pick up an eBook copy <u>right now</u> at Amazon!

Also By

MORE BOOKS BY C.H. JAMES?
Want more? Yes, please!

Instalove Short Reads:

Curvy Girl Getaway – Steamy Soccer Romance
Broken Promise
Spanish Secret
Kiss at Midnight
Rebound Suite
Curvy Girl Getaway Series BOXSET

Curvy Kilts – A Scottish Highland Romance Series
ANDREW – My First Love
ROBERT – My Older Man

The Locker Room Series – A Steamy Hockey Romance Series
My Curvy Puck
Captain's Curvy Puck
Puck My Roommate
My Virgin Puck

My Grumpy Puck

The Locker Room Series – Books 1-4 BOXSET

Operation: Curvy - A Navy SEAL Series

Sealing Her Fate

Operation SEAL Her

Surrender To Her

Her Curvy Explosion

Falls Creek Falcons – A Bad Boy Hockey Romance Series

Bad Boys: Shut Out

Bad Boys: Game Over

Bad Boys: Pressure

Bad Boys: Hard Play

Mountain Men of Falls Creek – A Wild Alpha Man Romance Series

Curvy Cabin

Curvy Camper

Curvy Christmas Collection – A Steamy Holiday Romance Series

Santa's Sack

Billionaire's Naughty Elf

Full Length Novels:

HATE The Game – Oaks East Vipers - Book One

HATE The Player – Oaks East Vipers – Book Two

About the Author

STEAM. ALPHA. HEA.

INSTALOVE.

Bestselling author C.H. James writes short, spicy, addictive stories. Escape the real world in exotic locations with hot heroes and relatable characters. There is ALWAYS a happily ever after, leaving you satisfied and hungry for more.

A steady stream of new releases will keep you busy, so please follow C.H. James by signing up to the newsletter at: https://bit.ly/chjamesnewsletter